The
WHITE
ROOM

a novel

JEFF GEIGER JR.

Jan-Carol
Publishing, Inc

"every story needs a book"

The White Room
Jeff Geiger Jr.
Published November 2021
Little Creek Books
Imprint of Jan-Carol Publishing, Inc.
All rights reserved
Copyright © 2021 Jeff Geiger Jr.

ISBN: 978-1-954978-31-7
Library of Congress Control Number: 2021950396

You may contact the publisher:
Jan-Carol Publishing, Inc.
PO Box 701
Johnson City, TN 37605
publisher@jancarolpublishing.com
www.jancarolpublishing.com

For Brandon and Cyndee.

You two are immensely missed.

Prologue

Three and a half years ago, I sat in front of a police officer I didn't know and told him about the worst time of my life. He needed a written statement of everything that took place in the White Room—a place that I'll never forget for as long as I live.

After I finished the written statement, my dad told the man that I used to write short stories in high school: primarily fiction. I never won anything, but my mom loved reading them. She would give me a few dollars per short story, and I would write one to three per week sometimes. And after the third or fourth story, I found that I enjoyed the process of writing fiction more than the money she would give me. Unfortunately, she died from an aneurysm while depositing mail at the post office. It tore me apart when I discovered my mom's unexpected passing, and I haven't written any stories since. I was in my junior year of high school, and at the time it was the worst thing that had ever happened in my short life.

Until the White Room.

Although, that particular room isn't the only one in that hellish place that keeps me up at night while everyone else is sleeping.

Before I tell you about that, though, I should tell you about my psychologist, as he's the one who suggested I write all this. His name is Bill Streetman, and he told me I should write my story. (My dad also told him about how I used to write when I was younger. I suppose I have dad to thank, as well.) He told me to tell the whole story—not the abridged version like I did for the police, but the real one. The one that tells all. He told me that if I did, there was a good possibility it would help me with some of the things I was going through, the insomnia being the worst.

At lunch one day, Bill leaned forward and said, "When you can't sleep, Jonah, break out the laptop and go to town. Get it all out. Delete it when you're done if you want to, but for Pete's sake, get it out."

I understood what he was thinking, or hoping for, anyway. People write in diaries and journals for a reason: it keeps them from bottling up their grievances and problems.

As I sit here at the kitchen table, sipping on a beer in a pair of old shorts, I've decided to write again. Bill's right, as he often is, and he's always there when I call him at two in the morning to talk about things. Maybe I owe it to him, and if not, maybe I owe it to myself to give it a try.

When I can't decide on whether to do something or not, I often think about what my mom would say in times like these. Although she isn't here, I can still hear what she would always tell me when I wasn't sure about something: *You can do this, Jonah. Go for it, honey.*

Chapter 1

I left my house that day on my metallic-blue motorcycle, a Harley-Davidson Sportster. My dad wasn't fond of me getting one, but I used the money I made working a little more than part-time at Lenny Ashmore's Handyman Service, so he couldn't argue the fact that I had earned the death trap fair and square. I knew part of it was just that he feared losing me like he lost Mom.

It was a balmy Sunday around noon when I threw one leg over my Harley. I was sitting astride a V-twin engine that shook the entire bike. I'd bungee-corded my skateboard to the sissy bar and was off to the skate-park to put my body—and well-being—in even more danger. I was nineteen and felt like nothing could hurt me. Nothing at all.

As the Florida sun worked its way out from behind a cloud, I flipped the tinted visor down on my helmet, released the clutch lever, and wrenched back on the throttle. The sound the bike made as I took off not only put a smile on my face, but it also made me forget all my troubles... for a little while, anyway.

I came up to a four-way intersection, and over the rumble of my motorcycle, I heard an even louder engine. It was a large truck, and its occupants were four obnoxious guys—they seemed like they were the my-dad-has-a-lot-of-money type of blowhards—shouting invectives at me from their heavily modified off-road vehicle. One of the guys in the backseat threw a beer bottle out his window, and it hit my helmet hard enough to shatter the bottle into a thousand minuscule pieces. It dazed me for a few seconds, and I almost tipped the motorcycle in my disoriented state. However, I stopped myself from hitting the asphalt and scraping the side of the tank. By the time I was able to focus and see straight again, the truckload of assholes was flying down the road away from me.

The skatepark was just to my right, perhaps fifty yards from the stop sign where I had been struck in the head. I saw Zane Kellington, my best friend, rushing out of the park and toward the parking lot. I rode over and met him near the front entrance.

"Jonah! Are you okay?" he asked me when I shut the bike off.

The helmet muffled some of the sound, but I was still able to make out his question. "Yeah, man, I'm good. Do you know those guys?" I asked as I took off the helmet.

"I know the guy who threw the bottle. He was up here yesterday doing stupid stuff like that to some guy just walking down the street with his dog, except yesterday he threw the beer bottle at the dog. I think his name is Greg. From what I've heard, he and his dad moved to Tampa just recently."

"What kind of piece of shit throws beer bottles at dogs?"

"The same kind of piece of shit that throws beer bottles at a motorcyclist, Jonah."

"Good point."

"You sure you're okay?"

"Yeah. I mean, I think so."

"I guess we'll find out when you get on your board."

"I guess we will."

We skated the concrete-bowl section of the park and did our best to enjoy ourselves as usual. After thirty minutes or so, we sat at our favorite picnic table under the park's pavilion. We were the only ones there at the time. Zane looked at me and smirked as he pulled out some rolling papers and an herb that resembled oregano. Everything was going great; we were having a good time.

Zane had just finished rolling us one up when I heard what sounded like the large truck that I had unfortunately encountered earlier. I'd be lying if I said I wasn't a little scared. Four guys who had money to get them out of trouble versus two skinny skaters with no interest in using the gym while in high school. The odds were not in our favor. We saw them coming, and Zane immediately put the weed back in his pocket. We grabbed our boards, as they were all we had to defend ourselves with if the blowhards came at us with more beer bottles. The four guys jumped down from the monstrous truck. Each one had a beer bottle in his right hand.

Greg, the one who'd thrown the beer bottle at me earlier, was fit and tan, and he apparently fancied mullets, as he had one. His cronies were also fit, except for the chubby shorter one in the back of the group, and each crony was sporting the same 1980s hairdo as Greg. I looked at Zane and laughed until my stomach began to hurt. All fear had left me at the sight of these four guys with mullets in the twenty-first century.

In retrospect, maybe I shouldn't have laughed, because soon after I was being slammed on the ground. The fit-and-tan Greg tackled me and started throwing punches. I dropped my board and blocked the punches the best I could. He didn't land many on my face, but he did get in a few good blows to my abdomen. While on the ground, I looked over to my right and saw two of them on Zane. He still had his board and seemed to be using it to block most of their strikes. I couldn't see the chubby one, and at that point I didn't care; I was too busy trying to get that lunatic off of me.

Seconds went by, although it felt like minutes, and I heard another vehicle pull into the parking lot. The chubby crony shouted at his friends, but they either couldn't hear him or they didn't want to stop pounding on us. I tried to listen, but I wasn't able to make out what he was saying with everything going on. Then I felt a hard blow to the side of my ear. With my ears ringing, I began to wonder just how badly we were going to be beaten before they finally stopped.

A while after Greg struck me in the ear, he turned around to see why his chubby friend was yelling. To Chubby's dismay, three guys had gotten out of a mid-sized sedan and were rushing into the park. One of those guys was my little brother, Corey, who was wielding a baseball bat. His friends Sam and AJ walked up with him and were wielding baseball bats of their own. The three sixteen-year-olds were on the high school baseball team and knew very well how to swing for the fences. They were soon face to face with the cohort of mullet-sporting hooligans. They brandished their bats and made them run away from us and back to their large truck in a hurry.

"Thanks, Core. I've never been so glad to see you," I said, and I meant it.

"Of course, Jonah, but why in the hell did those guys pick a fight with you two?" he asked.

"They started it by throwing a beer bottle at me while I was on my motorcycle."

"Yeah. Then they left and came back. Seems like they had nothing better to do than beat up on guys they outnumber," Zane added.

When I looked over at Zane, I noticed he had a bloody lip. We'd been hurt worse while skating over the years, but seeing him injured because of a few idiots with a random desire to do harm just made me angry.

"You okay?" Corey asked me.

"My ribs are a little sore from getting blasted by that jerk, but I think I'm all right. I just need to sit down for a few minutes."

"Yeah, me, too," Zane said.

We walked over and sat at the picnic tables underneath the pavilion again. My ears finally stopped ringing, and we talked about what everyone was doing later that night.

"I hear Heather Rainey is having a big shindig at her parents' house tonight," AJ said.

"She's so fine. I swear, dude, tonight's the night I'm making out with her. You watch and see," Sam said.

"Pfft, Sam, you know her boyfriend isn't going to let you get within three feet of her," Corey said. "The guy is a monster and gets super jealous. That's a dangerous combo there, Sam, my man."

Zane looked at me and said, "Jonah, I don't know about you, but your boy Zane could definitely use a good helping of hot-girl party tonight. You in, man?"

"Yeah, come on out. I'll get you guys in, big bro," Corey said.

Truth was, I just wanted to go home, maybe drink a cup of coffee or two and get lost in a good paperback novel, then try to forget about getting my ass kicked by a few guys with mullets, of all things. But that wasn't what your average nineteen-year-old skater was supposed to be doing, right?

Damn, I hated stereotypes.

In the end, I decided I might as well go since Zane and Corey really wanted me to. I owed Corey one, anyway, for saving my ass. "Yeah, I guess I'll go."

"Sweet! This is going to be sick," Zane said.

"Just don't be getting in any fights tonight," Corey said, dropping me a wink.

"Believe me, the last thing I want to do tonight is fight."

"You guys want to get some batting practice in before the party tonight?" AJ asked.

"Hell yeah, I'm down," Sam said.

"Let's do it," Corey said. "I guess we'll see you guys later at the party."

"We'll see you guys there. For sure," Zane said. "I'm heading home to get a shower and grab some grub. Shoot me a text when you head out, Jonah."

"You got it, man. I'll see you tonight. Glad we didn't die."

"True that, my friend. True that," Zane said.

Corey, Sam, and AJ put their bats in the trunk of Corey's car. Zane threw his board in the back of his red Honda Civic and took off. I sat astride my Harley once more, started it up, and rode back to my house to drink coffee and read a few chapters before going to Heather Rainey's party.

Chapter 2

I put my novel down and started getting ready to go out when my dad entered the room. Ever since Mom had passed, he'd been extra worried about me and Corey. Especially Corey.

"Headed somewhere tonight, Jonah?" my dad asked.

"Going to a party with Corey and Zane."

"Oh, Corey didn't tell me that when he was here earlier. Don't you let him drink any alcohol or do anything that's going to get him hurt or in trouble. He has a bright future ahead of him. His coaches are already saying he's college ball material."

Usually, the older brother was the star athlete, the favorite, and the one most likely to excel. But in my situation, that wasn't the case. Corey surpassed my baseball skills his first year playing, even though I had already been playing the game for some time. Kid was a natural. I didn't resent or envy Corey. Honestly, he deserved to be the favorite.

"Don't worry, Dad. I'll keep a close eye on him," I said, and I recalled the fact that he had just saved my ass earlier that day. Like I said, he deserved to be the favorite.

"You be careful, too, Jonah, especially riding that damn motorcycle."

"I'm always careful, Dad."

"Son, it's not you I'm worried about. It's all—"

"...these damn other people out on the road around me, right?"

"Yes, that's right. Just, please, be safe."

"I will."

"Okay, well, I'll be here if you boys need anything. Take care of Corey."

On that day, I thought it was redundant for him to keep telling me something I planned on doing anyway. Caring for a younger sibling is an innate characteristic that remains dormant until an older sibling receives the news that he or she is going to be a big brother or sister. The fact that it's instilled in you by your parents your whole life also plays a key role. Later in life, I realized that was why Dad always reminded me.

I nodded impassively at my dad as I walked past him and out of the house.

It was during conversations like that when I really missed my mom. She always had a better way of saying things. Much more graceful and not nearly as abrupt. I knew he meant well. It was just not the same when I was used to having the be-safe lectures for years and years from my mother, who was conversationally gifted.

As I opened the front door and proceeded outside, I noticed the westering sun still hovering above the old oak trees across the street. My motorcycle stood there on its kickstand, under the shaded side of the concrete driveway, waiting for me to grab it by the handlebar grips and start it up. I was traveling at a speed of fifty miles per hour, and as the Harley and I pierced through the air in front of us, I felt happy again and disconnected from all of life's problems. I figured God made motorcycles loud for a reason; the noise drowned out the rest of the world.

Unfortunately, though, in this world careless people existed. A particular careless person was driving a large truck, much like the one I'd seen earlier that day. I was coming up on an overpass in Tampa, and as I rode under it, the large truck swerved into my lane. With only a second or two to react, I jerked the Harley to the right. By merely an inch, maybe less, I got around the truck and wasn't forced to jump the curb. (I would have been apt to lose control once airborne if my front tire had rammed the concrete curb. And at the speed I was going, if the crash somehow hadn't killed me, I'd have been in severe pain with at least a few broken bones.)

After I made it past the truck, I pulled into the first store entrance that I could. I put the bike in neutral and put down the kickstand. I turned to the left to look back in the direction of the incident. The truck was long gone; however, I had a good idea of who was in it. Looking for a fight at the skatepark was one thing; vehicular manslaughter was far worse. Perhaps they thought it'd be funny to mess with me by swerving in my lane, but I could have been killed. I considered going to the local police department and filing a report. I knew it was Greg and his three cronies, but I had no way of proving it beyond a reasonable doubt. I decided to save myself the time and effort.

I took deep breaths. I was trembling from the anxiety, but with the Harley vibrating like mad, no one would be able to notice. After gaining my composure, I raised the kickstand with my left foot and got back on the road.

As I cruised on, I started to relax again, but I was more aware of my surroundings than I had been before the truck nearly struck me. I was getting close to the address Corey gave me, and I realized I'd forgot to text Zane that I was on my way. I hoped he would be there already, along with Corey, Sam, and AJ. The navigation on my phone showed that I was one minute away from my destination.

Not long after that, I saw Zane's Honda Civic parked beside Corey's car, which was next to a two-story house, along with about twenty other vehicles. I pulled in and parked the bike next to Zane's Honda. When I took my helmet off, I heard a loud, harsh mixture of music and shouting from the house. My first thought was that her parents were not home and that the cops would be here breaking it up before the night was over. I proceeded to the front door, where a group of high school kids were out front smoking cigarettes and talking about how much they hated their teachers. They gave me a scornful glare as I walked by, as if I had a week-old dead fish tucked in the waistband of my jeans. I went to knock on the front door and missed; it moved inward before my knuckles could tap the wood. I recognized the two guys who greeted me. Each of them wore a smirk and looked like red-faced versions of my brother and Zane.

"I see you two have started without me," I said.

"Come on in, big bro. Let's get you a drink," Corey said.

"Yeah, man, join the party," Zane added.

"How did you guys even know I pulled in the drive?"

"We could hear your Harley, duh," Zane said.

"Over all the noise? When did you guys get supersonic hearing? Also, how do you acquire such an incredible ability?" I asked, displaying a smirk of my own.

"A few beers, that's how. Here, Jonah," Corey said, handing me one.

This wasn't the first time Corey drank in front of me. I'd gotten the bum down at the gas station by our house to buy us beer a few times, but I'd never seen him this drunk before. It worried me because my dad was right. Corey had a bright future ahead of him. I didn't want to see that ruined. Being the nineteen-year-old who did nothing productive in life was my thing, anyway.

After accepting the beer from my brother, I asked, "Core, how many have you had?"

"Just two."

"Plus another two," Zane said.

"Okay, four. It's not a big deal. I'm going to ride this buzz out the rest of the night," Corey said.

"That would be best. But think about it, Core. Loud music, underage drinking, cars parked all over the place. The closest neighbors only like fifty yards away. You know this is going to end with the cops shutting the thing down. And if they shut it down soon, guess who's too drunk to drive: you," I said.

"Jeez, you sound like Dad."

"He's just looking out for you. Lighten up," Zane said.

"I don't need him looking out for me. I'm the one who came and saved your asses earlier today, wasn't I?" Corey said to Zane, then rested his eyes on me. "Do me a favor and let me have a good time. Okay? Thanks."

Corey walked off, and I began to go after him, but Zane put his hand on my shoulder to get my attention and said, "Just let him go cool off, man. I tried to get him to slow down, but that Heather chick just kept handing him beers. She gave him a shot, too. He told me not to tell you."

"Well, thanks for telling me. Just keep an eye on him for me tonight, Zane."

"Yeah, man, of course."

"Have you had much to drink tonight?"

"Nah, not much. This is my first one," he said, holding the beer up. "You of all people know I prefer the sticky green stuff."

"I know. Just checking. I'm going to find another drink. Call me if Corey gets too stupid."

"Will do, man. I'll let you know where we're at when I find him."

"Thanks, Zane," I said, then headed toward where I surmised the kitchen would be, but I ended up in a room full of partygoers playing beer pong.

When I entered the room, I noticed that there was a hole in the far wall, as if someone had punched it or perhaps fallen into it in their drunken stupor. There were two tables set up for beer pong, with several inebriated teenagers shouting and getting immensely excited about tossing a ping pong ball into a red plastic cup. Needless to say, I wasn't drunk enough to share their enthusiasm.

I proceeded through the crowd and made it into another room that wasn't the kitchen. To my left and right, couples kissed and felt each other up under their clothing. I was beginning to wonder just what kind of party this happened to be. I walked briskly to the next room, avoiding awkward eye contact with the kissing couples.

The next room I entered turned out not to be a room at all; it was a hallway that led to my desired destination: the kitchen. The cherrywood cabinets, granite countertops, and stainless-steel appliances looked like nothing I had ever seen in a house before. Only on television and in magazines had I seen such opulence. On the granite counter next to the humongous French-door refrigerator, I saw several rows of pre-made shots just waiting to be consumed. I didn't plan on getting drunk, but if I was going to stay at this party for more than five minutes, I needed a couple shots to make it easier to deal with the people around me. After the two shots, I opened the fridge door and found it teeming with beer. I grabbed one and sipped on it as I made my way out of the kitchen to look for Corey and Zane.

I walked into the dining room next. Someone had pushed the dining room table and chairs into one corner. I surveyed the room as partygoers came and went as they pleased. Corey and Zane were not present, but Heather and her huge boyfriend were talking to each other about something that I couldn't hear over the music and chatter.

When I stepped foot into the next room, my stomach sank as I saw Greg and the mullet squad surrounding my brother and my best friend.

Chapter 3

I knew I should have stayed home. I could have continued reading my Dean Koontz novel and had a nice, quiet night before work the next day.

When I saw the goons standing there with Corey and Zane, my first thought was, *Shit, this is going to end badly.* My second was, *Where the hell are Sam and AJ?* And my third was that I owed those bastards for running me off the road earlier.

The alcohol finally hit me, and it hit me hard. I didn't know what kind of shots they were, but in retrospect I probably should have only had one. Or none.

I jumped when I felt someone's hand grab my shoulder. Sam and AJ were behind me, and we saw what would be another unfair fight in the other room if we didn't do something about it. They each held a bottle in their hand, as did I. Without speaking, we all knew what we had to do next.

I ran in first, and Sam and AJ came rushing in right behind me. By the time I reached Greg, he and the chubby crony were on top of my little brother, throwing wild punches at Corey. I hit Greg in the back of the head with my half-drunk beer bottle as hard as I possibly could. He fell to the floor next to Corey and lost consciousness. Fortunately for me, the bottle remained whole, allowing me to use it on Chubby next. However, Chubby saw Greg snoozing on the tile floor and made a beeline for the door before I could club him with it. I looked over to see if Sam and AJ were doing okay, and they were. Both of their bottles had broken, and the remaining cronies were lying face down with golf-ball-sized goose eggs on the back of their heads.

I reached down to help Corey up. As I pulled him to his feet, I noticed his eye was beginning to swell. "You okay, Core?"

"Yeah, I think so. Luckily, I can't feel a whole lot right now. Did you hit him with a beer bottle?"

"Yeah, I did," I said, then looked down at Greg, who was still snoozing on the floor.

"Jonah, come here, man," Sam said.

I saw them hunched over Zane. I told AJ to keep an eye on Corey, and then I bent down to examine my best friend's injuries. His nose was bruised and possibly broken. He was conscious but disoriented and unsure about where he was at the moment.

As if things couldn't get worse, from another room in the house, I heard the chubby crony shout, "Hope you like jail, because I called the cops for what you guys did with them beer bottles."

At first, I could not believe what I was hearing. The situation was so absurd that I almost began to laugh. But there wasn't any time left for that. We had to get out of there as soon as possible. I needed to get Corey home before he got caught drinking underage, but first we had to get Zane to the hospital.

"Sam, are you okay to drive?" I asked.

"Yeah, I didn't drink anything tonight. I planned on being the designated driver for Corey."

So, Corey did have a plan, I thought to myself, then felt bad about lecturing him earlier that night. "Okay, good. You and AJ need to take Zane to the hospital to get him checked out. See if you can get the keys out of his pocket and take his car. I'll drive Corey's car and meet you guys at the hospital."

In my alcohol-addled mind, that plan sounded good, at least until I got behind the wheel of Corey's sedan. Despite the adrenaline coursing through me, the immensely strong shots of alcohol I'd ingested earlier had my head spinning. One thing I stayed fixated on, though, was that I had to get Corey out of there before the cops arrived.

I put the car in reverse, nearly hitting Heather's mailbox, and peeled out of the driveway.

In the yellow glow of the car's headlights, I spotted Sam, AJ, and Zane up ahead of me. I followed them out to the main road. To get to Tampa General Hospital quicker, we would have to take the interstate. They seemed to already know this and headed toward I-275, saving me from calling them.

It appeared that we had made a successful escape and had avoided the local police. But then, before we were able to take the on-ramp, I looked up and saw flashing red and blue lights in the rearview mirror. Corey and I looked through the rear window at the white police car.

I was in big trouble.

I was somewhat reluctant to pull over, but I did after I gained the courage to do so. I watched as Sam, AJ, and Zane continued up the on-ramp and disappeared onto the well-lit highway. To my right, Corey was becoming frantic. He had never been in any real trouble before. Luckily for him, I was behind the wheel and, if we were caught, it'd be my ass with a DUI. On the shoulder of the road, I left the motor running. I flipped the overhead dome light on, rolled my window down, and had Corey give me the registration and proof of insurance.

As he handed me the papers, I said, "Be cool. We'll be okay, all right?"

He acknowledged me by shaking his head up and down in short, quick movements. He didn't say anything. I thought that if he had, he might have lost his ability to hold it together.

In my side mirror, I saw the police officer get out of his cruiser. As he walked toward us, his flashlight blinded me for a short time when its intense brightness reflected in the mirror. I blinked my eyes several times, trying like hell to regain my vision.

To my left, the police officer asked, "What are you boys up to tonight?"

I could see a little now, but my vision was still blurry. I said, "Just headed home, sir. I had to pick my brother up from his friend's house. He's really sick."

"Is that right? You sick, kid?" he asked my brother.

My vision came back just in time for me to see Corey shaking his head up and down again without speaking. When my eyes rested back on the cop, I saw that he was a tall, dark-skinned man who looked as if he could be on the cover of a fitness magazine.

I handed him my license, registration, and insurance papers without him asking me to do so. My nervousness was palpable, and I knew he could smell the alcohol on both of us.

He took everything I handed him and smirked. "Sit tight, Mr. Bosworth," he said, reading my license. "I'll be right back."

I watched as he ambled back to his cruiser, steeling myself for what was going to happen when he returned.

Corey finally found his voice. "Jonah, what's going to happen? Do you think he knows we've been drinking?"

"No, I don't think so," I lied.

"Well, why do you think he pulled us over, then?"

"I don't know, Core. Maybe I was going two miles over the speed limit and he was bored. Let's just play it casual and see what happens."

"Yeah. Okay. Casual. Right."

"Corey?"

"Yeah, Jonah?"

"Do you know what was in those shots on the kitchen counter?"

"Moonshine, why?"

"That explains a lot."

I heard the squeak of the cruiser's door opening. The police officer was walking back to the driver's side window. This time, he didn't blind me with his flashlight, and I was able to make out the letters on his gold nameplate as he approached: M. Welkins.

"Well, everything checks out just fine with your paperwork," Officer Welkins said, handing the papers back to me. I handed the papers to Corey, and when I looked back around, Officer Welkins was smirking again. He looked over at Corey, then rested his eyes on me and asked, "Now, do you boys know why I pulled you over in the first place?"

Corey and I shook our heads as if we had no idea what we had been doing wrong that night.

"Look, guys, I've been doing this job for a while now, and I'm not stupid. Dispatch just came on the radio and informed us that a fight broke out at a party in the area. One with an abundance of underage kids drinking alcohol. I can see that you boys are scared, and I can also smell the booze on you two."

At that point in time, I seemed to lose the ability to produce words. My head was spinning not only from the alcohol I had consumed but also from the imminent world of shit I was about to enter. I glanced over at Corey and saw tears slowly rolling down his cheeks.

I really wished I would have just stayed home and read my damn book.

After five seconds or so of neither one of us responding, Officer Welkins said, "So, as much as I hate to have to do this, you boys know I have to take you in, right? Mr. Bosworth, you're not even twenty-one, and you're driving under the influence. Please step out of the car."

I did as he instructed. He had me walk to the front of the vehicle.

"Turn around and place your hands on the hood of the car."

I continued to obey his instructions. Next, he cuffed me and patted me down. I looked through the windshield at Corey. He was looking at me through the tears that coursed down his cheeks in rivulets. I saw him say something to me. I couldn't hear it, but I was able to make it out by reading his lips.

"I'm sorry, Jonah. I'm so sorry."

Chapter 4

As I was being placed in the back of the cruiser, I began to wonder what he was going to do with Corey. "Sir, what's going to happen to my brother?"

"Well, he wasn't driving. I'll have to get your parents' phone number from you or him and have them come pick him up. After you see the judge, they can bail you out if they want to do so."

"I can give you the number. It's my dad's cell. My mom isn't with us anymore."

"I'm sorry to hear that, son. I'm sorry about all of this, but it's my job."

"I know," I said, then gave him the phone number.

Officer Welkins closed the cruiser's door and began to call my dad. I would never hear the end of it, but at least Corey wouldn't get in much trouble. Everything was just how it was supposed to be: Jonah, the screw-up son, and Corey, the son with the bright future.

I sat in the back of the cruiser, hands cuffed behind my back. I thought that perhaps he did that because it was protocol, or perhaps he did that because he thought I might try to run away. That thought *did* cross my mind, but the repercussions would undoubtedly be far worse than just a DUI charge.

What a day this turned out to be.

Minutes later, a white Ford truck pulled up behind the cruiser. It was my dad. The red and blue beacons on the top of the cruiser illuminated his face as he looked at me sitting in the back of the police car. His disgust and disappointment were easily readable as his eyes rested on mine. After he made his disapproval on the matter clear, he cast his eyes down toward the ground as if he couldn't stand to look at me any longer. I watched him walk away with his hands in his pockets, still looking at the ground, most likely pondering where he went wrong with me. He met with Officer Welkins over by my brother's car. They conversed for a few minutes while Corey remained seated in the passenger seat.

I saw more flashing lights behind me. It was a tow truck. The driver backed up to the front of Corey's car, slid the hydraulic wheel lift under the frontend, and drove away with it.

After the tow truck left with the car, my dad, Corey, and Officer Welkins began walking toward me. My dad didn't even look at me as he walked by the police car. Corey's eyes met mine for just a second or two. The skin around his eyes was red from crying, or maybe it was only the red from the cruiser's beacon.

Officer Welkins opened the door and sat in the driver's seat. He began to fill out something on his laptop. "You know, your dad is pretty upset with you, kid."

"Yeah, I gathered that."

"You know in Florida there's a Zero Tolerance Law for underage drinking and driving, right?"

"No, sir, but I know now. How long will I be in jail?"

"Well, kid, if your blood alcohol level is over 0.02, you're looking at anywhere from two days to six months."

My stomach nearly sank into the seat when I heard him say six months. "How do we know my blood alcohol level is over 0.02?"

"Well, we don't yet. But I can smell the booze on your breath, you see, and that gives me probable cause to make the arrest. And I know you boys left that party that just got busted. I've been following you since you turned off the road leading to that house. Now I can administer the breathalyzer test, if you'd like to see if you're under the legal limit."

Thinking back to the shots and beer I had earlier that night, I felt that I'd fail miserably. "And if I pass?"

"Then I'll simply drop you off at your house. You'd be free to go."

My mind began to race. I knew that if I took the test and failed, a lawyer couldn't help me in any way. But I felt sober then. I didn't know if it was the anxiety sobering me up or if I was just thinking I was sober because I was still intoxicated. In the end, though, I decided it was my only shot at getting out of the situation and not going to jail. So I took it.

Officer Welkins got out of the car and opened the rear driver's side door. He took a small device out of its carrying case, turned it on, and positioned it in front of me. "Okay, kid, so you just blow on this plastic piece until the beeping stops. Got it?"

I nodded and began to blow. It wouldn't register at first. Then I began to blow harder.

After a few seconds, the beeping stopped.

Looking at the breathalyzer's screen, he frowned. "Sorry, kid. It's .083."

I closed my eyes and took a breath, letting it out slowly. I was on the verge of tears when I felt an immense rush of wind blow past my left side. I shrank back from the rear driver's door and closed my eyes once more, this time turning my face away from the door. There was a brief, muffled grunt, followed by the sound of something large hitting metal. When I opened my eyes again, Officer Welkins was gone. A car had run him over.

Chapter 5

I was hesitant to move. I couldn't believe what I had just witnessed. I didn't *want* to believe it.

The car that hit him appeared to be black in color, but I was unable to be sure with it being so dark out. The car just sat there, fifty feet or so in front of the cruiser I was still sitting in, idling and not moving.

In the back of the cruiser, I sat with my wrists still cuffed behind my back, the interior light on, and the door wide open. I looked at the spot Officer Welkins had been just a few seconds ago and spotted a clump of keys. One of them had to fit the cuffs. My first thought was to grab the keys and run like hell, but I had to call this in; I had to do the right thing.

I edged my way toward the end of the seat. When I stood up, I tested my flexibility, seeing if I could at least maneuver the cuffs to where they'd be in front of me instead of behind my back. I began by sitting back down, positioning my arms in a way that created a circle for my legs to go through. Thanks to my long arms and suppleness, I was able to bring my cuffed wrists in front of me. Then I bent down and procured the keys, stuffed them into my front pocket, and grasped the front driver's side door handle. As I pulled it open, I saw the laptop. Next to it was the radio, which I could use to call dispatch and inform them of what had transpired.

Before I got the chance to reach for the radio, I heard something coming from in front of the cruiser.

"Who's over there? I hear someone," the unknown man shouted.

I didn't say anything in return, mostly because I didn't know what to say. I was scared, and I had no clue what to do.

"Hey! There's someone in the car. Quick, get him before he gets away," the unknown man said to his accomplice.

As I heard their footfalls getting closer, I was able to see, in the cruiser's headlights, that one had his knife out. The other seemed to just be ready to take out any witnesses with his bare knuckles. They were still a good forty feet in front of the cruiser, and I didn't waste any time getting the hell out of Dodge. By the time they made it to the cruiser, I was already in the woods next to the side of the road.

I didn't look back. I ran and I ran until I needed to stop to catch my breath. Hunched over, with my elbows propped on my knees, I lifted my head and looked around me. Nothing but woods and darkness. The only light was that of the moon and stars. I wasn't sure how long I had been running, but I didn't see or even hear the two men who were looking for me. It seemed I had made a successful escape. At least, I hoped I had.

The crickets chirped all around me. The sound was actually quite soothing. I had lived in Florida all my life, and strangely that sound had never quite served me like it did on that particular night.

Soon, after I managed to catch my breath, I realized the severity of my current situation. I got a DUI. However, the officer who gave me said DUI was apt to be dead. I wasn't able to call it in and do the right thing. If I had stuck around to do so, long enough for those two louts to get ahold of me, I'd probably be buried in the woods somewhere.

I sat down with my back against a thick, gnarled trunk of an old oak tree. I dug the keys out of my pocket and began trying each one until I found the key that unlocked the cuffs. When I tried the fifth one, I felt the cuff loosen around my wrist. A sigh of relief escaped me, and then I unlocked the other cuff, stood up, and threw them deep into the dark woods. Now I had to figure out what my next move would be.

What I had been caught doing was bad. There were no ifs, ands, or buts about it. I messed up big time. Yet my DUI seemed to be a harmless transgression compared to what the two guys in the black car had done. I sat there for what felt like five hours, although it was only twenty minutes, contemplating what I should do next. I knew what the right thing to do was, but I also knew they wouldn't come looking for me like they would the two guys who had struck Officer Welkins. Eventually, I convinced myself to walk a few miles back to Heather Rainey's house. My hope was that my Harley was still there, so I could ride it back home to my cozy bed. It was the only plan I could come up with.

Thanks to my smartphone, I was able to find the shortest—and quickest—route back to Heather's. I used the flashlight on it to help illuminate the area in front of me. After twenty-six minutes of walking, according to my phone, I had made it to the paved road that led to Heather's house. I began walking up the tarmac drive. The streetlights' yellow glow gave the road an ominous feel that made my arms break out with gooseflesh. I felt paranoid that either the police would come rushing at me in their squad cars, guns drawn, or that the two men would come after me to make sure there wouldn't be any witnesses to speak at a future trial, if there happened to be one.

Roughly a hundred yards in front of me, I saw Heather's house. The music had been turned off, and there were only two lights on in the whole place. As I got closer, leaving the woods behind me, I saw that there was still a police cruiser parked next to the front door. He was probably waiting for her parents to get home before leaving the house. I hurried back to the woods I had just left. I needed to be as inconspicuous as possible, so I stayed on the edge of the woods, keeping out of the light emitting from the streetlights until I reached her yard.

My Harley was still next to a few cars that had also been left when shit had hit the fan earlier that night. My night had not been a lucky one, but there was an SUV to the right of my motorcycle, concealing my Harley from the cop's view. First, I walked as stealthily as I could manage in my semi-intoxicated state. One moment, I'd feel sober because of the adrenaline coursing through me; the next, I would almost fall over from loss of balance. After almost losing my balance for the second time, I sidled over, not quite army-crawling, but staying low and out of the police officer's sight. Soon, I made it to the Harley, and as I threw a leg over it and put my helmet on, I thought of something I should have realized a while ago: *How the hell am I going to get out of here undetected with a loud exhaust that can be heard from half a mile away.*

I needed to think of something—and fast—because behind me, through the clear shield of my helmet, I saw headlights coming in my direction. As the vehicle made its way down the road toward me, its intensely bright headlights blurred my vision for a short time. It seemed to be my night for having bright lights impair my vision. As it got closer, and as I regained my ability to see once again, I recognized the vehicle from earlier. It was the same truck that had almost run me off the road: Greg and his godawful cronies.

This night just kept getting worse and worse, or so I thought at the time. What I didn't know then was just how much worse it was going to get.

The truck's custom dual exhaust issued a deep, throaty sound as it approached me. All of a sudden, a light bulb began to flicker in my head. I realized that with the roar of the truck's engine, my motorcycle wouldn't be as noticeable if I started it and made a break for home. By the time this registered in my brain, the truck was only about eighty feet from me. I had the ignition turned on, my headlight illuminating the area in front of me, and without hesitating any longer, I pressed the start button. The engine roared to life on the first try. I dropped the transmission into first, and as I popped the clutch with my left hand, I wrenched back the throttle with my right. Grass and dirt flew up into the air from my rear tire as the bike lurched forward. I whipped it around, shooting past Greg and his cronies, making my way toward the end of the road before the police officer could put two and two together. As I passed

Greg, I wasn't pelted with beer bottles. They did throw a few—they just all missed me this time. I rode away unscathed, and I figured that, rather than simply trying to hit me with bottles again, they were also getting rid of any evidence that they had been drinking. Talk about killing two birds with one stone.

I checked for traffic to my left and right before zipping out onto the main road. The ride home was chilly, especially for Florida in late March. I checked my mirrors, and to my surprise there wasn't a large truck chasing after me. Maybe Greg had finally had enough of me, at least for tonight.

I headed home, thinking about everything that had happened on this horrible night. After remembering that Zane was on the way to the hospital, I couldn't allow myself to go home before making sure he was okay. I pulled over on the shoulder of the road, placed my phone on the cell phone mount attached to the handlebars, and turned around. I rode my chrome, screaming deathtrap back the way I had just come.

Up ahead, where I had previously been pulled over that night, were three police cars and an ambulance. One of those police cars was the one I had been sitting in the back of earlier. Police officers were shining their flashlights into the woods and searching for evidence. The guys in the vehicle that had struck Officer Welkins were long gone. My hope was that they focused more on the guys that struck him and not me. But I felt that at some point I was going to have to face the music. Although I didn't feel good about my decision, I rode by as if I had no clue what was going on and got on the on-ramp. I merged onto the interstate, following the directions that the GPS had given me. There was only one thing on my mind: getting to Zane and making sure he was okay.

I pulled into Tampa General a few minutes past eleven o'clock. Quickly, I parked the bike in the ER parking lot and jogged toward the entrance, taking my helmet off as I ran.

When I entered the building, I saw Sam and AJ sitting in the corner of the waiting room. "How is he?" I asked, hurrying over to them.

"Don't know, man. They haven't told us anything," Sam said. "He's been back there for almost—"

Behind me, a light-brown door opened. A nurse and Zane came ambling out. He looked like he was fine, but his tan nose was bruised worse than it had been earlier. The nurse helped him over to where we were in the corner of the waiting room. She helped him sit down and looked at the three of us.

"Your friend here is lucky he didn't break his nose. He just needs to ice it a few times a day. The bleeding has already stopped. However, the bruising may continue to get even worse," the nurse said, then glanced back at Zane. "Also, Mr. Kellington, you'll want to do your best not to sneeze. It would be incredibly painful, and bleeding could reoccur. If it does, do not tilt your head back. Just let the blood come out and use a napkin or tissue to absorb it. Any questions?"

We shook our heads, conveying that we didn't have any.

"Very well, then. You boys try not to get in any more trouble tonight." She turned around and went back through the light-brown door, and I saw Sam checking her out as she exited.

"Zane, I'm glad you're good, man, but you gotta tell me something. Did you get a smooch or two from that goddess, or no?" Sam asked.

"Sam, shut up," AJ said. "Zane, how you feelin'?"

"I'm okay, guys. I mean, my nose feels like Dale Earnhardt ran his racecar into it going two hundred miles per hour, but I'll make it."

"Feel dizzy at all?" I asked.

"Nah, not anymore. I'm good. Say, I thought you got pulled over earlier. I guess you got out of it somehow?" Zane asked me.

Failing to come up with a believable lie, I said, "It's a long story, man. I'll fill you in on it soon. We're good, though. I just wanted to come make sure you were okay."

"Aw, Jonah, you're such a sweetie," Zane said, pinching my cheek and laughing.

"Okay, keep it up, Kellington, and you'll have a black eye to go with that bruised nose of yours," I joked.

"Okay, you two, play nice," Sam said.

"Let's get out of here," AJ said. "I'm tired and ready to go to bed."

We all began walking toward the exit. It was close to midnight, and a number of things were on my mind. I was still worried about what my dad would say when I got home. I didn't have a believable excuse for why I was home and not behind bars. And on top of that, I had work first thing in the morning with Lenny Ashmore.

In the hospital's parking lot, before I went over to where my Harley was, I called Zane over for a quick chat as Sam and AJ continued walking toward Zane's car. He could tell by the look on my face that I had something serious to tell him.

"What's up, Jonah?"

"I messed up."

"Messed up what? What are you talking about?"

"It's a long story."

"Yeah, you mentioned that earlier. Dude, whatever is going on, you can tell me."

I cast my eyes down at the pavement and said, "I'm kind of on the run from the cops, I guess."

"You guess?"

I glanced up and saw Zane scratching his head and locking his wide eyes on mine. "You see, while I was sitting in the back of the cop's cruiser, he was struck by a random car. I'm pretty sure they killed him. The two guys in the car got out and started walking toward me. When I noticed that one of them had a knife, I ran, man. I didn't know what else to do."

"Are you messing with me?"

"I wish I was," I said.

He turned around, still scratching his head. A few seconds later, he faced me again and said, "You've got to go to the cops and tell them what happened."

"Then I'll definitely get a DUI."

"That's better than leaving the scene of a homicide done by two guys who were obviously bad people. Jonah, what the hell are you thinking, man?"

"I don't know. I'm just scared, and the alcohol clouded my judgement. I was actually going to call it in to dispatch, but before I could get to the radio, the two guys were getting close."

"Jonah, you have to go to the police department. Maybe you'll get a DUI, and maybe you won't, but if you get caught up in this later on, it'll only make matters worse. No good can come from you hiding and acting like nothing ever happened."

I felt like an idiot for being so reluctant to do the right thing. Zane was right, though. He usually was, that one. "You going to still be my friend if my mugshot gets blasted all over social media?"

"Dude, you know I would," he said, chuckling.

I sighed and said, "Well, I guess there's no time like the present, right?"

"Go do what you have to do, man. I'll go with you if you want me to."

He was my best friend and had been since the ninth grade. We had each other's backs, but tonight I felt I should face the music alone. "No. It's cool, man. I appreciate it. Just come bail me out if my dad ends up refusing to, okay?"

"You got it, man."

I walked back to my bike and threw a leg over it. I saw Zane get in his Honda. At that moment, I had no idea that it would be days before I saw him again.

Chapter 6

I put the Tampa Police Department's address into my phone and hit the button that would display three different routes to the station. Since I was on my motorcycle, I chose the scenic route. It would have less traffic, and it would take longer to get there, which was good since I was in no hurry to turn myself in.

I turned left out of the hospital and, after five miles, took a narrow road that veered off to the right. It led out to a road consisting of nothing but open fields on either side. Although, after another five miles or so, instead of open fields, to each side of the road were vast acres of land covered with trees. I had never ventured down this particular route before.

As I cruised at a smooth fifty miles per hour, the only light was that of my motorcycle's headlight. Out here on this long stretch of two-lane blacktop, there were no streetlights or side roads. It was a straight arrow to the other side of town, and it would be ten miles or so before I'd make it there, according to my phone's navigation.

I tried to stay calm as I continued down the long stretch of asphalt, but as I put mile after mile under my heels, I began to feel nervous and downright afraid of what they would do to me when I got there. I had never been in a situation like this before. I supposed a multitude of people hadn't been in this kind of situation before.

Lucky them.

I kept thinking of what I would say when I got there. I wasn't sure where to even begin. Perhaps they'd let me write it all down instead of putting me in a room, sitting down in front of me with a tape recorder, and having me explain what took place that night. I was not even sure my vocal cords would work or produce words in that environment. I'd never been the best public speaker.

Writing was always my preference for informing or communicating.

The clock on my phone struck midnight, and this new day wasn't any better than the previous one. I was still on my way to the station to clear my name and tell the police what really happened, even if I was charged with a DUI.

As I cruised on, trying my absolute best to enjoy the ride and not worry about the inevitable, I spotted a girl lying on the side of the road up ahead. I kicked the shifter down with my left foot and slowed to a stop ten feet away from her. I left the Harley's headlight pointed directly at the girl. It was the only source of light I had other than my phone, which remained fastened to the motorcycle's phone mount.

The girl was passed out on her side, not moving or making a sound. Her pungent perfume smelled of coconuts, and she wore a gothic-style outfit with fishnet leggings, along with shiny black combat boots. From what I could see, the makeup on her face seemed thick, but it was partly concealed by her long black hair and her left arm. Her right arm remained by her side.

"Ma'am, are you okay?" I asked.

No response.

I took my helmet off and noticed she was holding a syringe in the hand by her side. She seemed to have a firm hold on it, even in her uncon-scious state. I feared my night would become even more complex now that I had discovered a dead girl on the side of the road who appeared to have overdosed. For some reason, instead of immediately calling the police, I bent down to check for a pulse. I wasn't a nurse, doctor, or even a dentist, but I put two fingers on her wrist—the one that was covering her face—and checked for a pulse anyway. To my surprise, she had one. And what was even more of a surprise was that her eyes shot open in a glare of contempt, and she tried to stab me with the syringe in her other hand. I dropped my helmet as I sidestepped her attempt to stick me with the needle, then grabbed her wrist with my left hand. The needle came close to penetrating my skin a few times as I tried to wrestle the syringe away from her with my right hand.

"Calm down," I said. "I'm not going to hurt you. I was just checking to see if you were alive."

"Liar!" she yelled as I wrenched the syringe out of her hand and took a few steps away from her.

I saw a clear liquid within the syringe. I had no idea what was in it, but it was full, and I knew I didn't want it injected in me. I threw it in the woods to ensure that she wouldn't get a second chance to stick me with the mysterious drug.

She bared her teeth at me and looked utterly insane as she said, "You worthless idiot. Go fetch my Midazolam this instant, or prepare for the most pain you will have ever experienced in your miserable little life."

I had no idea what Midazolam was, but she did appear to be addicted to the drug. An addict who would resort to physical violence if she couldn't get her fix. I had had enough crazy for one night, so I decided to run back to my bike and get the hell away from the lady. Seemed like a good enough plan until I noticed two big, burly men standing next to my motorcycle. One of them was Hispanic, and the other was Caucasian. Both men were covered in black and gray tattoos. In the scant light, that was all I could make out. Judging by the scowls on their faces, they didn't seem to be the cordial type.

"Who are you?" I asked the two men.

The white guy, who had a long dark-colored beard, stepped forward and said, "We're salesmen."

"Yeah, and I'm the prince of England," I said.

"No, really, we are," the Hispanic man, who I noticed wore an eye patch over his right eye, said.

I glanced behind me quickly and found that the goth girl was gone. The two men were still standing by my Harley. I asked, "What do you sell, then? And where did that girl go?"

"Insurance," the white guy with the beard said, ignoring my second question.

"So, why are you here?"

"Because you need insurance, vato," the Hispanic guy told me.

"Insurance for what?"

"For this," he said, pushing the bike over.

The right-side mirror broke into several pieces, the handlebars bent inward, and the tank was dented in from the impact with the asphalt. I became livid as I watched the motorcycle I had laboriously worked for be pushed over on its side in such a deliberate way. I wanted to rush them and bounce their heads off the pavement, but I was also terrified these two strange ogres would kill me if I tried to do just that.

"See, vato, you never know when you'll need insurance."

I felt my fingernails digging into the skin of my palms, creating little white crescents. I looked at my bike and then back at the two goons. I didn't know what to do. This wasn't exactly a situation I had ever been in before. My first thought, besides attacking them, was to call the police. It was not a bad idea, except that it would take them at least ten minutes to get to me. I figured I had better start thinking of a way to stall them. But I soon realized the problem with my plan as my eyes rested on the rectangular device attached to my Harley's handlebars: my cell phone. It wasn't damaged, but how I was going to retrieve it without the two goons stopping me, I didn't know.

The Hispanic guy smiled at me as if he had done me a favor by pushing my motorcycle over, causing damage I didn't have the money to fix. The white guy began to laugh at me, and that made me even angrier. But what could I do? I couldn't count on Corey and his friends getting me out of this one like they had before. Perhaps, like Greg and his cronies, these two goons only wanted to beat me up. I was beginning to believe that I had a face that certain people just wanted to harm. I decided to give them what they wanted. I saw no way of getting out of this unscathed.

"Okay, I get it. You guys just want to rough me up, destroy my possessions, and have a good night by making a fool of me. Is that right?"

"That's not entirely true," the bearded white guy said. "We want you to come stay with us, as our guest."

"What the hell are you talking about?"

"We want you to come *stay* with us. What part of that did you not understand, string bean?"

Ignoring yet another nickname the two had given me, I asked, "Why would I stay with you? You guys just pushed my bike over. None of this makes any sense. You guys told me you were salesmen, and now you want me to stay with you. Seriously, what's going on?"

The white guy glanced over at the Hispanic man with the eye patch. When he met my eyes again, he smiled and said, "Well, aren't you just a confused little string bean? I'll say it in a way you will definitely understand: *You* are going to *stay* with *us*."

"That's right, vato, and I see you been eyeballin' that cell phone of yours. You want it, don't you? Well, come get it. We don't bite," the Hispanic guy said with an eerie smile.

Something inside me, perhaps intuition or the fact that it was so clear that these two were looking for trouble, told me to get the hell out of there. I didn't want to stick around and find out what plans they had for me. It was time to run away and try to lose them in the woods. I was just about to turn around and make a break for it, but before I could, I felt a sharp pain in the side of my neck. I began to feel sleepy within seconds. I couldn't see who had provided the sharp pain, because my vision began to blur, but I did smell something just before I passed out: *coconuts*.

Chapter 7

I became semi-conscious for maybe five seconds—just enough time for me to realize that my arms were cuffed behind me and rope was tied around my ankles. I was in the back of some sort of sport-utility vehicle. The two goons were in the front seats, driving me to God knew where. Then I was out again, and I had a dream.

In the dream, I was dressed in the baseball uniform I had worn years ago, when I was perhaps twelve or thirteen. It was one of the last years I'd played little league. I remembered because I had gotten a skateboard for my birthday, and that was all I'd wanted to do since receiving the gift. I heard my name being called from the parking lot behind me. It was my mom. She closed the car door and began walking toward me with my tan baseball mitt.

"Your glove, sweetie. Can't forget it. You'll need it for the game today."

It was a dream based on a day that actually took place years ago. I'd had a game against the best team in the league, and we were taking team pictures that day right before the game. I was starting pitcher and as nervous as a med student administering an IV for the first time.

After team pictures, my mom pulled me aside and wanted me to take a few pictures with Corey. Corey's game started fifteen minutes before mine. My mom would walk back and forth between our games to watch us both the best she could. My dad wasn't there that particular day. He often had to work and miss our games, but Mom was always there to cheer us on.

I walked to the field my team was to play on. We did our warm-ups and took our positions after the national anthem. I took the mound and struck out the first two batters. The third batter, a kid who looked more like an eighteen-year-old, ambled up to the batter's box. I knew of the kid. He was very competitive and had had an early growth spurt, which wasn't good for me. After my windup, I threw the baseball as hard as I could. The big kid swung and hit a line drive that cracked me upside the head. Everything went black for a while, and then I woke to my mother's voice. I saw concern in her kind eyes as she looked down at me. But what happened next took me by surprise.

Mom grabbed me, her hands on my shoulders, and whispered in my ear, "Jonah, these people are going to hurt you. They're terrible human beings. You have to run, sweetie. Run as fast as you can. Do you understand? Please run."

Her voice began to fade away, and I realized I had woken up again. I was in the back of the sport-utility vehicle. The white guy was slowing the vehicle to a stop, and the Hispanic guy, who was riding shotgun, was ironically holding a shotgun in front of him, the barrel pointed down toward the floorboard. They looked back at me and saw that I was now awake. Awake, but still loopy from whatever had been injected into my neck.

"Ah, sleeping string bean is up. Say, string bean, are you going to cooperate with us now and come on inside?" the white guy said.

"My mom told me to run," I heard myself say. I didn't know why I did. Maybe because I was still loopy from the injection.

The Hispanic guy laughed and looked at the white guy. "Hey, Bruce, you hear this guy? His mommy told him to run. Man, she must have given him quite the dose."

"It appears she did, Enzo," Bruce said. "Let's try this again, string bean. Are you going to cooperate, or are we going to have to do it the hard way?"

I could barely keep my eyes open. Everything in front of me was spinning and making me nauseated. When I didn't respond, Enzo slammed the butt of his shotgun against the side of my head hard enough to knock me out again.

When I woke up the next time, I found myself untied and sprawled out on a paper-thin mattress. My head felt as if I'd really gotten hit by that baseball in my dream. I was no longer loopy, but I was scared. I lifted my aching head up from the thin mattress to view my surroundings. The lights were off. I was surrounded by pitch black. The only thing I could see were four blinking red lights in each corner of the room. Judging by the distance between the small red lights, the room itself wasn't very big. I had no idea what time it was, where I was, why I was there, or how I would get out.

A huge wave of fear shot through me, and I sat upright on the mattress, trying to control my breathing. I didn't want to start sobbing like a child, but I damn sure felt like doing just that.

To my left, I heard something move. My eyes shot in the direction from which I'd heard the noise. I still couldn't see anything in the darkness, but I did hear a small girl's voice.

"Hello?" she said softly.

"Where am I?" I asked, my voice just above a whisper.

"A bad place. What's your name?"

"Jonah. What's yours?"

"Milly. Are you okay, Jonah? Have they taken you back to their White Room yet?"

"I don't think they have. The last thing I remember was being tied up in an SUV. The Hispanic guy hit me in the head with his gun, and then I woke up here."

"That's Enzo. He and Bruce are the guards who work here for the doctor."

"Doctor? This can't be a hospital."

"It's not a hospital. It's—"

"It's hell," said another voice farther to my left.

Before I could ask, Milly said, "That's Ronnie. He's been here longer than me."

"These people, they ain't right in the head," Ronnie said. "Sooner or later, y'all will end up in the White Room, I'm afraid. I wouldn't wish what them people did to me on anyone." He coughed hard a few times after he finished talking, and it sounded painful. I couldn't see him, but I was almost positive that he had tears in his eyes.

After a few moments, I asked, "What'd they do to you?"

"Son, let's just say it ain't pretty. For now, we'll leave it at that. In time, you'll see for yourself. It was Jonah, right?"

"Yes. Jonah Bosworth."

"Well, Mr. Bosworth, I know Milly's story, and she knows mine. So, what's yours?"

"What do you mean?"

"How'd they find you, son?"

"Oh. I stopped when I saw a woman lying on the side of the—"

"Then Enzo and Bruce went over and stopped you from gettin' in your car. Am I right?"

"Well, from getting back on my motorcycle."

"I got ya. Then I reckon that woman on the ground jabbed a needle in your neck. Am I still right, son?"

"I take it that's what happened to you, as well, Ronnie?"

"Sure is. That woman is the dev— " He began coughing again. This time, he sounded even worse.

"Are you okay, Ronnie?" Milly asked.

After a few seconds, he said, "I'm fine, darlin'. I just need some water, but it ain't time for them to bring it out."

"It must not be seven a.m. yet," Milly said.

"Nope, not yet," said Ronnie.

"What happens at seven a.m.?" I asked.

"Go ahead and tell him, darlin'. I'm gon' rest my voice a minute."

Milly said, "At seven a.m., they turn the lights on and bring us breakfast. It's nothing that yummy. Most of the time, they just bring us water, a couple slices of bread, an apple, and sometimes chicken broth."

"Sounds like that would get old really fast," I said. Then, when no one said anything after a short time, I asked, "So, Milly, how'd you end up in this place?"

Ronnie coughed a few times, then said, "She doesn't much like to talk 'bout it, Mr. Bosworth. No offense."

"No, it's okay. Jonah was nice enough to tell his story," she said, then paused for a moment. "I went to a park in downtown St. Petersburg with my parents. The sun was just starting to go down, and I had to go to the bathroom, so my mom went with me. I finished before her and walked out of the bathroom to look for my dad, but I didn't see him anywhere. He had been showing me how to fish earlier, so I figured he must have been down at the lake still. Anyway, when I turned around to go back into the bathroom to find my mom, Enzo was standing right behind me. He grabbed me, put one hand over my mouth so I couldn't scream, and forced me into a black van. He held me down in the backseat while the doctor gave me a shot. Then everything went black, and I woke up here."

"I'm so sorry to hear that," I said, thinking about how terrifying that had to have been for her.

Ronnie said, "Don't worry, darlin'. I'm—" The coughing kept him from continuing, and it just kept getting worse. I hadn't seen the man yet, but he sounded terrible.

"Thanks, Ronnie. You should rest your voice, though," Milly said.

"Does anyone know what time it is?" I asked.

Milly said, "No, but when the lights get turned on, you'll see there's a clock on the wall by the door. It's a...what do you call it again?"

"Analog clock," Ronnie said, his voice hoarse.

"Right. Sorry, Ronnie," she said. "Ronnie isn't sure, but by watching the clock, his guess is that he has been here around a month. He's not sure how many days he was back in the White Room, though. They kept him on that laughing gas stuff. He doesn't remember everything that happened, I guess."

"Did he say what they did to him in the White Room?" I asked.

"He thinks they took out one of his kidneys."

"Why in heaven's sake would they do that?"

"I—"

The lights turned on. It took a few seconds for my eyes to adjust to the brightness, but when they did, I feared I would die here with these people.

Chapter 8

I surveyed the room and found five steel-barred cells, including the cell I was in. There were a few feet of space between each individual cell. Inside each one was a toilet, sink, and bed. The porcelain toilet and sink were covered in a layer of dust as thin as the mattress on the prison-style bed. I noticed the toilet's porcelain lid was missing. They weren't stupid enough to leave us with such a harmful weapon, unfortunately.

There was a door directly in front of my cell. It was the only door in the entire room. It seemed to be the only way out, because the room was windowless. I saw that the red blinking lights in each corner were actually surveillance cameras fastened to the sage-green walls.

In a cell to my left was the man I had come to know as Ronnie. I saw him lying in bed, holding his side. It appeared to be wrapped up with some sort of gauze, but a little bit of blood was seeping through the bandages. He looked to be in his mid-to-late thirties. His beard was thick and long, his shirt and shoes were missing, and his pants were covered in filth. I thought he might have been a little far off with his guess for how long he had really been in this place.

Next, I saw that the small dark-skinned girl, whose hair was in a pony-tail, was staring at me. Her clothes looked like they hadn't been washed in a week or two. She wore no bandages and appeared to be very healthy, unlike Ronnie in the cell down at the end.

"Well, what do you think?" Milly asked me.

The impassive look on her face told me that she had given up hope. She believed this was to be her life until she died.

"I think maybe we should come up with a plan for how to get out of here," I said.

"There ain't no way out, boy. If you go through that door, you're dead. And if you're not dead, you'll be back here in a cell, like I am now," Ronnie said. "Wish they'd bring our damn breakfast. I could use some water."

"Are you able to get water from the sink, or does it not work?" I asked.

"Ain't used the sink yet, have you? Give it a try."

I turned toward the sink and twisted the knob. A brownish liquid came out, spitting and sputtering. Startled, I turned it down until just a gentle stream flowed from the faucet. I ran my hand under the lukewarm water. It felt dirty and was in no way drinkable.

"I see your point," I said, looking back at Ronnie.

"Yep. So how do you s'pose we get out of here? You really think you can come up with somethin'?"

"I don't know. But we have to try, right? If we do nothing or don't try, we have no other option but to sit back and wait to be killed."

"Now I see your point, son."

"Ronnie, if you don't mind me asking, what'd you do for work before you arrived here?"

"I was a rancher. Grew up in the business. My father passed away a year ago, and then I took over. Why'd you ask?"

"Just getting an idea of the skills we all have. Can't start a plan until we know what each of us does well."

"Ah, I see. What is it that you do for work, son?"

"I'm a handyman. I work for Lenny Ashmore. He's the well-known handyman in my town. He says I'm the best worker he's ever had, though. That I have an aptitude for fixing things."

"I ain't ever heard of the man. I'm sure he's a nice feller."

"He is. So, what about you, Milly? Do you have any talents that may help us get out of here?"

She was looking down at the concrete floor, hands clasped together behind her back, thinking to herself. When she clearly thought of something, she glanced up and said, "You wouldn't believe me if I told you."

"Of course I would. Why wouldn't I?" I said.

"You won't, though."

I saw tears developing in her eyes. "It's okay, Milly. You don't—"

"Rise and shine," Bruce said as he opened the door. "How'd everyone sleep? Good?"

I looked to see if Milly and Ronnie were going to say something. They didn't, and neither did I.

"Well, isn't that swell?" Bruce said. Then his eyes shifted in my direction. "String bean, have you had a housewarming party with your new neighbors yet?"

I shook my head to indicate that I hadn't.

"I see. Well, don't worry. You'll have plenty of time to chat amongst yourselves. I'm sure you'll have some fascinating conversations, especially with farmer Ron over there," he said, using his thumb to motion toward Ronnie.

"I'm a rancher," Ronnie corrected.

"Who cares, you idiot," Bruce said. "You both smell like crap all day. Speaking of crap, what's that smell? Farmer Ron, don't tell me you made a mess in your trousers like an infant. You're a sad excuse for a man—and a farmer!" He burst out laughing and pointed at Ronnie like he was some kind of circus clown.

Ronnie bit his lip and stared at the area of concrete in front of him.

I couldn't hold back any longer. "Hey, it's Bruce, right?" I asked.

His gaze shifted back to me. "Yeah, string bean, it is. What's it to you?"

"I was just going to mention that it didn't smell like crap until you ambled in here looking like a bearded rodent."

His face morphed into a confused scowl.

To really throw gas on the fire, I asked, "Are you in pain, or is that just what you look like when you're trying to think?"

His skin tone reddened. He got the keys out of his pocket, opened my cell, and rushed in. I didn't run, mostly because there wasn't anywhere *to* run. I put my hands up to block his punches, but his right hook connected with my left eye anyway. I fell back against the porcelain sink, and I held on to it to keep from falling to the ground. My eye was throbbing, and I suddenly wished I had kept my mouth shut.

"Okay, I'm sorry," I said.

He grabbed me by my throat with one of his huge hands, lifted me up off the ground, and slammed me against the steel cell. I was sure this was the end of my short stay here.

"You're lucky Doctor Truex has other plans for you, or I'd crush your windpipe right now."

"Understood," I said, still covering myself, waiting for him to hit me again.

"Pissant," he said, then turned around and exited the cell. It was obvious that he wasn't worried about me striking him from behind when he turned around. However, he was wary enough to remember to lock my cell before leaving the room.

My eye continued to throb, and my back felt like someone had just struck it with a steel chair. I felt a little relieved when he left, but then the door opened again, and Enzo walked in the room. He carried a plastic tray that held three bottles of water, six slices of bread, and three apples. He put the food in front of Milly's cell first, and then he placed Ronnie's food in front of his cell. He approached mine last.

"Listen, vato, I know you're new here and everything, so let me tell you what's up. I bring the food in the morning. Then around noon I bring some more. Then around dinnertime I bring out the last meal of the day. If you don't like the food, you don't have to eat it. ¿Comprendes?"

"I comprendo."

"Good. I'm glad you do. Don't look so glum, vato. You don't have to see the doctor today. Oh, and nice shiner," he said, pointing to my eye.

Enzo glanced over at Milly, who had grabbed her food and begun eating the bread over on her bunk. "Hey, you up today, Milly," he said.

Her eyes were those of a deer in a driver's headlights. "I'm up?" she asked.

"Yeah, girl. You get to see the doctor today. Doctor Truex is going to run some tests. She just wanted me to let you know." He smiled at her like he'd smiled at me when he pushed my Harley over. "Now you know."

He left the room through the same door he had entered. I was glad to see him go.

To my left, I heard Milly crying.

"I'm sure it'll be okay, sweetheart," Ronnie told her. "You jus' got to be strong."

"I-I don't know if I can be," she said.

"Ain't none of this fair, but I'll tell you somethin'. By the time you get back from seein' that doctor, me and Jonah gon' have us a plan."

She wiped away her tears with the palms of her hands and looked at me. "Is that true, Jonah? Do you really think you'll be able to get us out of here?"

"I'm sure we'll come up with something, Milly. I'll do my best to figure out a way out of here. *That* I can promise you."

"I believe you will. I can tell you really believe you can find a way out of this place."

"How can you tell?" I asked.

"That's what I was trying to tell you before Bruce came in. I can hear what you're thinking."

I almost laughed, but I didn't want to hurt the girl's feelings. Instead, I asked, "What exactly do you mean when you say you can hear what I'm thinking, Milly?"

"Well, kind of like how I know you don't really believe I can. I guess I'll have to show you like I had to show Ronnie."

I looked over at Ronnie, who was sipping on his bottled water. He stopped when he saw me looking at him, put the cap back on the plastic bottle, and said, "I know how it sounds, but the girl ain't lyin'. She's got a real gift from God."

"I can prove it to you," she said to me.

"How?" I asked.

"Well, when I first told you, you wanted to laugh, but you didn't because you didn't want to hurt my feelings."

I was a little freaked out that she knew that, but I was still skeptical. The look on my face must have displayed just that.

She looked at me with a slight smile. "Jonah, I know that freaked you out and that you're still not sure yet." She looked off to her left for a few moments, thinking. "I've got it. I want you to think of something. It can be anything you want to think about. I just need you to be thinking about it hard enough for me to hear or see it in my head. That's how my *know-stuff* works."

"Your *know-stuff?*"

"Yeah, that's what I call it. When I focus on what someone is thinking, I know the stuff they're thinking in their head. Okay, ready? Think."

I closed my eyes and thought of my mother.

It was my fourteenth birthday, and she was wearing a long red dress, her hair up in a bun. Everyone was singing "Happy Birthday" to me, but what I remembered most was her smiling at me as she sang. In that moment, life was perfect.

After I blew out the candles, I wished for a new skateboard because my old one was worn out and apt to break in half the next time I used it.

My mom said, "Hold on, Jonah. Let me go get your present from your dad and me. I'll be right back."

The present she and my dad had purchased for me wasn't wrapped, but it didn't need to be. It was what I had wished for after I blew out my candles.

Her face began to fade away into a vortex, swirling into darkness as the thought ended. I opened my eyes and saw a single tear rolling down Milly's right cheek.

"That was such a nice memory," she told me.

"You saw all that?"

"Yes. And I heard what your mom was saying. But I saw you. A younger you. Your mom was wearing a red dress and singing 'Happy Birthday' to you. Then you wished for a skateboard after you blew out the candles on your cake. The last thing I saw was your mom bringing out the skateboard you had wished for. It was all very sweet. She seems like a nice lady."

I couldn't believe what I was hearing. This girl really was telepathic. No one could make such an accurate guess. I was speechless.

"Jonah, are you okay? You look like you just saw a ghost or something."

I turned to look at Ronnie. He was still sitting down and gave me a look that seemed to say, *Crazy, I know. But it's true.*

I met Milly's eyes again. Her little smile was gone. In its place now was a look of sadness and uncertainty.

"Milly?"

"Yes?"

"If you can really read people's minds, what was Enzo thinking when he told you that you were up?" I asked.

"He wasn't thinking about what was going to happen to me. He was thinking about how he hit you with the gun earlier. He enjoyed it. It looked painful in his memory."

"Yeah, I have the knot on my head to attest to that."

"I don't know what they're going to do to me back there today, but I'm really scared. What if they cut me open like they did Ronnie?"

Ronnie coughed a few times, then said, "Sweetheart, you jus' be strong. My first time back to see the doc wasn't bad. She'll probably jus' weigh you, check your vitals, and ask you a few questions. I reckon it was more like a checkup than anything." He sounded a little better now that he'd had some water.

"I hope you're right, Ronnie," Milly said.

"Milly, I know you're scared, but you *do* have to be strong, just like Ronnie said. You have an incredible ability, and I believe—even more so now—that we can really find a way out and back home. It may take some time to get this plan just right, but we'll get there. We'll get Ronnie back to his ranch, you back to your parents, and me back—"

Bruce and Enzo came into the room. Bruce held a pair of handcuffs in his left hand, Enzo had overtly stuffed a 9mm pistol in the waistband of his chinos, and the two of them were making their way to Milly's cell.

Milly turned around and shifted to the far corner of the cell, her arms over her head in a protective manner. "Please, no. I don't want to go back there," she said.

I wasn't sure if she had read their minds and knew something we didn't or if she was just scared and panicking.

Ronnie spoke up. "It's okay, Mill—"

"Shut up!" Bruce said. "You say another word, and you'll be eating my fist for brunch."

Ronnie was furious, but he didn't say another word. By this, I gathered that he'd most likely learned to listen the hard way when he first arrived here. He knew Bruce meant what he said. Hell, I had learned that not too long ago myself.

Enzo entered her cell first and grabbed her arms, wrenching them behind her back. I wanted so badly to say something, to rush in and hit them as hard as I could, but I couldn't. I had to watch as they cuffed Milly, a small, defenseless girl, and forced her out of the room. She thrashed and thrashed as they walked her toward the exit. As she went through the door's threshold, she glanced back at me, and my eyes met hers for just a second before the door closed.

I was scared I'd never see her again.

Chapter 9

I could still hear her screaming in the hallway—or whatever happened to be on the other side of the door. Then, a few seconds later, I heard another door slam, and after that I could no longer hear Milly. I continued to stare at the door, unable to believe how cruel those two could be.

"Them two ain't got no souls," Ronnie said.

I shifted my gaze over to his cell. He was now sitting on his bunk, his head between his knees, looking down.

"I fear you're right about that," I said.

He looked up. "How are we goin' to get out of here?"

"I don't know yet. You've been here for a while now, right?"

"Yeah, too damn long. I'm surprised they ain't killed me yet."

"Why do you say that?"

"That lady doctor cut me open. Says it's to find a cure for the disease I have. I know I ain't got no disease, but that's what she keeps on tellin' me. To be honest with you, I want to say she took my kidney or somethin' out, but I really don't know."

"She had to have made the incision for some reason, right?"

"I reckon so," Ronnie said, then glanced at the ground again and started to cough. When he looked up this time, his eyes had welled with tears.

"You okay, man?"

His voice trembled as he said, "I have to tell you somethin'. I ain't told Milly this because I didn't want to scare her, bein' so little and what not. But you're grown, so I know you can handle it."

I nodded.

"A few days before Milly got here, there was a little boy 'bout Milly's age in that there cell 'cross from me. He was here before I got here. His name was Louis, and he was a good kid," he said, looking at the wall now, lost deep in his thoughts. "We had become good friends. We played I Spy and Charades to pass the time. He was good at them games, too.

"Well, one day he done got took back there by Bruce and Enzo to see the doc. He came back hours later with a cut that had been stitched up 'bout like mine. He was okay for a couple days, just sore from bein' cut open. Then one morning, I woke up and saw that he was havin' trouble breathin'. I hollered as loud as I could for help when Louis started gaspin' for air. Not long after I started hollerin', Bruce came in through that door. When he saw what was going on, he picked the kid up and ran out of here. I...I ain't seen Louis since then."

The tears that were in his eyes had fallen and now glistened on his cheeks. "I'm so worried about Milly. I can't handle seein' another innocent child die like that." Ronnie coughed again and looked back down at the floor. He brought one of his hands up and wiped his face. "I know you ain't been here long, son, but we have to think of somethin'. I hope you got some ideas, because I've been here a good while now, and I still can't figure out how to get outta this place."

"There has to be a way out. One way or another, I have to get out of this room to see the layout of the place. We could be in a small house that consists of only a few rooms, or it could be the size of a hotel. It could be a straight shot to a door leading outside or a labyrinth that would leave us lost for hours."

"Well, son, within a week you'll probably be out of this room, but it won't be for reconnaissance." It came out *re-can-a-scents*.

"Maybe I can fix something around here to show them I'm worth keeping around. I mean, think about it. If something breaks here, do you really think Bruce and Enzo are going to fix the problem?"

"You mean, like, if a toilet or somethin' breaks?"

"Well, yeah. I can fix plumbing, drywall, most electrical issues. You name it. See, I could show them that I'd be useful around here. They would be getting those things fixed for free, and I would be able to see the layout of the place. Once I see what we're working with, I may be able to come up with a plan."

"Dang, son, that's a darn good idea. How'd you come up with that so fast? You ain't even been here a whole day yet."

"I fix things. I've never impressed anyone in sports or academics, but I've always been able to fix things," I said, then looked at the clock on the wall. "But only time will tell if I can fix this mess we're in."

I began to look around my cell, thinking of ways to show these people that I could be an asset, not just some experiment for them to poke and prod away at. I paced back and forth, feeling Ronnie's eyes on me as I did so. He didn't say anything. Other than a coughing fit here and there, he was silent.

My eyes suddenly locked on the toilet. That would be my way of exhibiting my skills to them. The components inside a toilet's tank were quite simple to understand. One valve filled the tank with water. The other valve flushed the water down and then filled the bowl with clean water. I just had to hope Bruce and Enzo were as dumb as they looked and couldn't fix it themselves. It would be easy to disable either valve and then fix it, or I could even replace it if they'd be willing to get me the parts from the hardware store. Even if they wouldn't get me the parts, I'd be able to fix it and show the big dummies that they needed to keep me alive. Things around here had to break at some point. I could be their handyman just long enough for me to make an escape plan.

I walked over to peek into the toilet's tank. Through the brown-ish water, I could see that a blanket of rust covered the bottom of the tank. Its fill and flush valve looked old, and so did the flapper. I almost reached in to disable the flush valve, but I remembered that the cameras were on. I was being watched from four different angles. Already, I had almost ruined my plan. To keep them from getting suspicious, I lifted the plastic lid, took a leak, and flushed. The toilet did in fact work just as it should, which left me asking myself how I was going to disable it while I was being watched every hour of the day.

I heard something to my left. The sound of cards being shuffled. Ronnie had a deck of playing cards in his hands, and he laid them out in front of him on the concrete floor.

"What are you doing, Ronnie?"

"Playin' Solitaire."

"I see that, but where'd you get the cards from?"

"Ah hell, I forgot 'bout you bein' new here. Bruce lets us have somethin' to entertain ourselves with. It helps pass the time."

"It helps keep your mind off of figuring a way out of here, too."

Ronnie's forehead wrinkled as he considered what I had said. "I ain't never thought of it that way, but I reckon you are right 'bout that."

"What items do they let us have?"

"Well, cards, as you see here." He looked up at the ceiling, his hand on his chin, thinking to himself again. "Oh, they let you have crayons and colorin' books. I s'pose that's more for the kids, though." He glanced over at Milly's cell. "They have a dozen or so books that you can read, too, if you fancy a good story. Milly over there picked out some book 'bout how to eat worms or somethin' the other day."

"I love to read, actually. And that book you're talking about is called *How to Eat Fried Worms*. I remember reading it in elementary school. It was a fun one."

"Yep, that's the one. Last book I 'member readin' was *Charlotte's Web*. That was many years—" He coughed for about eight seconds and then drank the rest of his water.

"You okay," I asked.

"Yeah. I mean, my side here is sore a'course, but I think I'll be all right. I just wish I had more water. Gon' be tough waitin' till lunchtime."

I'd completely forgotten about the food Enzo had brought out. I reached down and grabbed the bottled water, took a drink from it, and put the cap back on. "Hey, Ronnie, can you catch this bottle if I slide it down to you?

His cell was about twenty feet or so to my left, on the other side of Milly's cell.

"Jonah, you don't know how much I'd 'preciate that kindness."

"Don't worry about it, Ronnie. I'm really not thirsty or hungry anyway."

He got down on the concrete floor, his arm stretched out of his cell. I aimed the bottle the best I could. However, when I slid it, it rolled onto its side and took off to the right. I thought he wouldn't be able to catch it, but Ronnie's fingertips just barely stopped the bottle from going off toward the two unoccupied cells.

"Whew," Ronnie said after procuring the bottle. "That was almost bad. Hey, thanks for this."

"Don't mention it. How long do you think Milly will be back there?"

He took a sip of water, then said, "My first time back took 'bout an hour, I reckon. They took a whole bunch of my blood. I got a soda after I got done givin' it, though."

"Man, this place is weird."

"I'd say. It's like prison but wor—"

The room's only door opened. I saw Bruce and Enzo escort Milly back to her cell. She had only been back there for maybe half an hour. I noticed a white piece of gauze taped to her left arm as soon as she walked in. Her movements were slow, and she kept her eyes cast down at the concrete floor as she took each step. When she got to her cell, she finally looked up, and I saw how red her eyes were. It appeared that she had been crying the entire time.

Bruce shoved her into the cell harder than he needed to. I stood up, and he looked me dead in the eyes. "You got a problem, string bean?" he asked me.

I did, but I also knew that I didn't stand a chance at doing anything about it without some sort of weapon to level the playing field. "No," I said, then sat back down on my bed.

"Good. You know what? I think I'm starting to like you, string bean. What do you say? You want to be my friend?"

I didn't acknowledge him.

"Hey, dipshit, I'm talking to you."

I looked at Ronnie. His eyes were large and round. He shook his head yes.

I took the hint. "Yes, Bruce, that would be nice," I lied.

"That's good, vato," Enzo said from behind him.

"That is good. Great, even," Bruce said. "So I expect you to comply from now on. You know, since we're friends now."

"Yeah, of course."

"All right, then. You kind folks will see Enzo here around lunchtime. Don't have too much fun in here without us," Bruce said, and then he left the room, Enzo following.

I looked back over and saw Milly lying face down on the bed, her hands covering her face. Seeing Milly cry only made me want to hurt Bruce more. I was going to ask if she was okay, but Ronnie beat me to it.

"Milly, you okay, sweetheart?"

"Yes," she almost moaned.

"Milly, are you able to tell us what happened? It may be conducive to getting us out of here," I said.

She lifted her head up and turned to look at me. Her face was slick with tears. "The lady they call Doctor Truex shoved a big needle in my arm and took my blood. It hurt a lot."

"What happened before she took your blood?"

"She asked me a bunch of questions."

"Do you remember some of the questions she asked you?"

"Some of them." She stopped crying and wiped her face with her shirt. "She asked if I was diabetic. I wasn't sure what that meant, so I said

I didn't know, and she slapped me. I cried, and she slapped me again and told me to stop being such a baby. After I stopped crying, she asked me if I smoked, and I said no. She asked a lot of questions, but the only other one I remember her asking was if I am allergic to anything. I told her I am allergic to peanuts and cinnamon."

"You're doing great, Milly. Are you sure you can't remember anything else she asked you?"

"I'm sorry, Jonah. I can't." She was about to start sobbing again.

"Milly, it's okay. You did great. You're being very brave," I said, and then to distract her I pointed to the book in her cell. "I saw the book you've got there. I've read that one before. What do you think about it?"

She went over to the book and ran her fingers along the cover. Looking down at it, she said, "Oh, um, it's interesting. I've read the first sixty pages so far. I can't believe the kid in the story wants that money bad enough to eat all those worms."

"I remember reading it in elementary school. I always liked that one." Then I glanced down at her arm. "How's your arm feeling?"

"It's sore. I just want to go home so bad right now."

"I'm right there with ya," Ronnie said. "Did they at least give ya some soda?"

"Yeah, when I got done, they gave me some. It was nice having something other than water."

This place was just so strange to me. I couldn't figure out why they had us locked up in here like zoo animals. They obviously took something out of Ronnie, but why? Was this doctor just practicing on us for some experimental reason? I also wondered what happened to the kid Ronnie had been friends with before Milly and I arrived. Was he dead? I had so many questions but no way of finding out the truth. Well, behind these steel bars I didn't.

That was going to be the key to finding a way out. I had to wait until the lights went off so I could disable the toilet. When I fixed it, I could only hope they'd have me fix other things for them. Finding a way out of here was probably going to take longer than I hoped, but what other choice did I have? While I waited, I needed to see about getting a book from Enzo when he brought us lunch.

"Jonah," Milly said.

I blinked a few times, coming back to reality after zoning out. "Yes, Milly?"

"Why are you thinking about a toilet?"

Ronnie started chuckling at the way she asked.

"I'd probably keep the toilet talk down," I said, having forgotten for a short time that the girl had telepathic abilities. Then I whispered, "They could be listening by the door or even with the cameras."

"Oh, they can't hear us through the cameras," she said.

"How do you know that?"

She gave me a you-know-I-can-read-minds look.

"Right, telepathy. Sorry. I'm new to this whole learning telepathy is actually real thing. Even though you've proved it, it's still difficult for me to wrap my head around. It's good to know they can't hear us, though."

"Mmhmm. So what did you guys come up with while I was back there?"

Ronnie said, "Jonah has a plan, but he can't do it till them lights go off."

I said, "Ronnie's right, but to be sure they don't hear the beginning of the plan, maybe you should just read my mind to understand the first phase."

"Okay, that's fine with me. Go ahead and think of it," she said.

I focused on the plan in my head, saying it over and over. After the second time I thought over the plan, she knew the first phase.

"Oh," she whispered. "That's why we have to wait for the lights to go out."

I nodded. "It should work as long as the cameras don't have night vision. Judging by how old they look, they are most likely not set up for that feature. And I'm sure they wouldn't trust anyone on the outside to update their cameras and keep hush-hush about what they're doing to people in here."

"You ain't heard them talk...I mean, think 'bout whether them cameras can see us at night, have ya, Milly?" Ronnie asked.

"No, I haven't. Most of the time, they think about money and what they're going to spend it on."

"We're just going to have to risk it. I'll do my best to make it seem like I'm just urinating, and I'll use my body to hide that I'm actually disabling it. Then, in the morning, I'll tell Enzo my toilet isn't working."

"What if you get caught, though?" Milly asked. "Then what?"

That was a good question. I wasn't sure what they would do to me, but I was sure it'd involve pain. Lots and lots of that. "Let's just hope I don't get caught."

Chapter 10

I watched as the clock's big hand ticked its way around and around until noon came. I didn't want to see Enzo, but I was getting a bit hungry. I also wanted to inquire about getting a book to pass the time until they turned the lights off on us. Watching the clock's big hand rotate was getting old, and thinking about everything that was going on just stressed me out to the point that I needed an aspirin.

I heard footsteps near the room's door. There was a *thud* just outside of the door, then an expletive followed by the sound of something else hitting the floor. A few seconds later, Enzo's ugly mug came through the door. He was holding a tray with our lunch on it.

"Hey, how's it hangin', you guys? Enjoying yourselves?" Enzo said as he set the tray down on the floor. "Your food may have a little dirt on it. Clumsy Enzo's balance is a little off today, I guess." He smirked at the three of us. "It's cool, mi amigos. You can always clean it in your toilet water."

He laughed and handed Milly her lunch first. It was the same meal we'd had that morning: bottled water, a couple pieces of bread, and an apple, all served on a cheap paper plate. The only difference was that this meal was covered in dirt. We all knew the apples would wash off, but the bread would just be soggy and covered in filth.

Enzo gave Ronnie his meal next. "Here ya go. How's that side feelin'?"

"It hurts like hell," Ronnie said.

"Want me to get you some pain meds for that, vato?"

"That'd be great. Can ya real—"

"Don't get your hopes up. I was just yankin' ya chain. The doc wouldn't waste pain meds on you, dummy."

Ronnie grabbed his food and water and turned away from Enzo.

"Ah, don't be mad. Remember, I'm the one who let you have those cards. You know, I can come in there and take those away from you if I want to. And you givin' me the cold shoulder like that kind of makes me want to take those cards, farmer Ron."

Ronnie sounded as if he were about to cry. "Please don't take my cards."

From the dreary look in his eyes, I could tell he felt helpless, sad, and just plain scared of what else was going to happen to him in this place. All he had was those cards. I was biting my tongue, but if Enzo took those damn cards away from Ronnie, I was afraid I would make the same mistake I'd made earlier with Bruce. Fortunately, Enzo wasn't in the mood to rip any cards out of a defenseless man's hands right then.

"All right. Calm down. I'm not goin' to take your cards, fool. But next time, you best respect Enzo, or else I will take those cards from you. Now say you're sorry."

"I'm sorry, okay?" Ronnie said, his voice still trembling.

"Good," Enzo said, then began walking toward me. "You hungry, Jonah?"

"You know my name?" I asked.

"Of course I do, vato. I know everyone's name in here."

"Right. My bad. Anyway, could I please get a book from you. I'd love to have something to read."

"Oh, sure, that's no problem. I just need you to do somethin' for me, okay?"

"Okay, what?" I asked.

The ends of his mouth curled up into a creepy grin. I didn't like what that grin suggested. Surely, it would be nothing good.

He slid my plate of food into my cell and placed the bottled water next to the plate. "You dip that bread into your toilet water and take a good bite of it for me, and then I'll bring out all the books we have. You can pick whichever one you want. How's that deal sound, vato?"

"Never mind," I said. "Forget it."

"Oh no. Now I want to see you do it, and Enzo always gets what he wants."

"And if I don't?"

"I'll come in there and make you eat it." He smirked. "So, what is it goin' to be, vato?"

I remembered reading somewhere that toilet water was supposedly cleaner than the human mouth, so to avoid the beating Enzo wanted to give me, I lifted the bread from the plate, submerged it in the toilet water that I had forgotten was brownish, and took a bite. The bread didn't taste too bad at first, but then, as I kept chewing, I felt the specks of rust—I hoped it was rust—crunch between my teeth. I tried to gather all the specks into one side of my mouth. When I felt confident I had done just that, I spat the rust back into the toilet and swallowed the bread.

"Open your mouth. Show me you ate it," Enzo said.

I opened my mouth, humiliated.

"That's sick. I'll be back in a few, vato. You crazy," he said, laughing as he left the room.

I threw the rest of the soggy, rust-covered bread in the toilet and flushed. I blew the dust off the other slice of bread and started to eat. I'd save the apple for last. To my left, Milly was steadily chowing down on her lunch. To the left of her, Ronnie had already drunk half of his water. He didn't seem to be very hungry, though.

"You okay, Ronnie?" I asked.

"I think so. I'm jus' not very hungry right now. It hurts to eat with whatever they done did to me. And Enzo bein' mean like that didn't help my appetite, neither."

"Ronnie, speaking of whatever they did to you, does it feel like anything inside of you is missing?"

"I really ain't got a clue. I wish I did. I don't know if they took somethin' out, put somethin' in, or jus' took a peek inside of me for some other reason. I jus' know my side hurts and that I'm gettin' tired. I'll prob'ly take a nap here soon."

"I understand, Ronnie. I'll let you get some sleep."

He nodded and turned on his side, facing away from me. I was worried about him not wanting to eat. That was never a good sign.

I noticed Milly lying on her bed, quietly chewing on her apple and reading her book. When she came to a stopping point, she said, "You know, you are kind of like the kid in this book, but instead of eating worms for money, you are eating toilet-water bread for a book."

I couldn't help but laugh at the irony, even though Enzo had basically forced me to eat the toilet-water bread. It was also hard to believe that I was laughing while confined in a cell against my will. It was a crazy world we lived in. My mother used to always tell me that. She could not have been more right.

"You know, you're not wrong," I said. "I know the toilet water looks bad, but it's actually clean. It won't make me sick or anything, but that's only because I spit the rust out."

"Either way, it's pretty gross," Milly said, smiling a little.

"Again, you're not wrong. At least I'll be getting something to entertain myself with. You think he'll really bring me a few books to choose from?"

"I do. He made Ronnie do one hundred pushups for his cards. That was before they took him back there for his surgery, though."

"Oh, I see. So, what did he make you do for the book you're reading?"

"He just asked if I wanted something to keep myself busy with. I said yeah, and he brought a few different things out. Then I picked a couple books."

"He didn't make you do anything for them?"

"Nope," she said.

"Well, I got ripped off. So, what was the other book you picked out?"

"Huh?"

"You said you picked a couple books out. What was the other one you chose?"

"Oh, I picked *Holes* by Louis something."

"Louis Sachar?"

"Yeah, how'd you know that?"

"I've read that one, too. It was one of my favorites when I was younger."

"Jeez, you've read a lot of books, haven't you?"

"I suppose I have," I said, then peeked at Ronnie to make sure he was still breathing. He was. "So, what did you do for fun before this all-inclusive stay at the world's worst hospital?"

"Mostly just gymnastics. I wanted to be in the Olympics one day, but now I'll never get that chance," she said, then started to cry.

"I didn't mean to upset you, Milly. I'm sorry."

She tried to say something, but all that came out were muffled syllables.

"Don't give up on that dream. I'm going to get us out of here. When they take me back, like they did with you today, I'll be making mental notes every second I'm out there. There has to be a way out, especially with those two dummies guarding the exit."

She stopped crying and met my eyes. "I know you really believe you can, and I really do, too. I just hope we have enough time for you to figure it all out."

I had to be careful about what I was thinking, or else she'd know I was worried about that same exact thing. Maybe she already knew. "Well, Ronnie's been here a good while. I think we'll have enough time. All we can do is stay positive, right?"

"Yeah, you're right. It's just hard."

"It is, but if we just keep acting like we're clueless, they won't get suspicious. We need them to be as careless as possible. That's the only way for this escape plan to work in our favor."

"I think I—"

The room's door flew open. Enzo was standing in the threshold, holding books and looking furious. I was certain he had heard us.

Chapter 11

When I was nine, I got in a fight during my physical education class. It wasn't really much of a fight, as it was a cheap shot to my abdomen. A bully named Richie Newton didn't like that I caught a ball he had thrown at me in the middle of a dodgeball game, causing him to "get out." So, to get even, he caught me by myself at the water fountain after the game. I felt my shirt tighten on my shoulders as he grabbed ahold of the fabric, turning me around to face him. He buried his right fist into my stomach. My lungs struggled to find an adequate amount of air, and the pain in my abdomen was tremendous.

Now, the look in Enzo's crazed eyes made me feel just like Richie had made me feel then.

Enzo walked in the room with the books, staring only at me. "What chu guys talkin' about, vato? Anything interestin'?"

I took a deep breath before I said, "Not unless you happen to have an interest in gymnastics."

He squinted at me as if I were speaking French, then became angry once more. "Don't give me that crap. You think this is a game?" Enzo asked.

Before I could respond, he ran up to my cell, dropping the books and grabbing the steel bars. I watched the veins bulge from his tatted arms and wondered if I was about to be killed.

He bared his teeth at me. "You lucky I don't have the keys, vato, or else I'd make you tell me the truth. You feel me?"

"Enzo, I swear we were—"

When he saw the apprehension in my face, he began to smile. I knew this guy was crazy, but I didn't know how crazy. He began laughing quite loudly, and after a good fifteen seconds or so, he said, "Chill, chill. I was just clownin' you, man. You got so scared. You don't need a new pair of underpants, do you?" He laughed again and hunched over, leaning on my cell.

Part of me was glad he was kidding and didn't overhear us; the other part of me was annoyed that he really did scare the crap out of me. Not literally, of course.

As I continued to stare at him, unable to believe he'd pull such a joke, he asked, "Whew, I really had you goin', didn't I, vato?"

"Yeah...yeah, you did," I said. "You should've been an actor."

"You think so? I've had some of my boys tell me that before. I would always play pranks, you know, and convince them I was serious when I wasn't."

"You should go for it. Hop on a plane and leave this place in the past."

"Aha, I like you, man. You got a sense of humor. But Enzo ain't goin' nowhere soon. I'm makin' too much of that green stuff here. You feel me?"

I didn't feel him, but I definitely construed what he meant when he said he was making *that green stuff*. Which made me understand why we were here. They had some sort of lucrative business—one where we were the guinea pigs and they were the ones reaping the rewards. Enzo and his colleagues were sick, but yet we were the ones waiting to see the doctor in this prison-like hospital.

I felt like he was telling us more than he was supposed to, which made me realize that he was easily the most careless one in their group. I did something risky, but I had a hunch it would go my way. I attempted to see what other information I could get out of this numbskull.

"Oh, well, I can't say I blame you for sticking around here. The doctor takes pretty good care of you. Is that right?" I asked.

"Yeah, that's right. I just bought a Subaru, one with a turbo, and that thing is fast as hell. You like cars, vato?"

"I do. That the all-wheel drive one?"

"You do like cars." He chuckled. "I knew I liked you, man. I'm almost sorry I made you eat that toilet-water bread. Oh, so get this. I'm goin' to put some rims on it soon. Going to be lookin' real nice."

"That'll be awesome," I said, faking enthusiasm. "Oh, hey, is what you said about not having the keys to the cell true?"

"Huh? Oh, yeah, Bruce holds the keys."

"That's kind of messed up, don't you think?"

"Well, he's been here longer than me, man."

"Oh, so it's like a seniority kind of thing?"

He pulled out his cell phone. "Yeah, I guess," he said, looking at the phone's screen. "Look, I got to go, man. You want to pick out a book real quick?"

"Yes, of course."

Enzo turned around and picked up the books one by one. He came back over to my cell and began to read them off. When he got to *Lord of the Flies* by William Golding, I told him that I would like to read that one. It was a novel I had read twice already, but I was not one to complain about revisiting a good story. Enzo handed me the book, not bothering to take any precautions. It was apparent that he didn't consider me a threat. He gathered the rest of the books and headed toward the door, leaving the room and then peeking back inside to inform us he'd be back at dinnertime. I heard him walking down the hall, and soon his audible footfalls faded away.

I looked over at Milly and asked, "Were you able to read any of his thoughts?"

She almost smiled when she said, "Not much. His thoughts change so fast that it's hard to keep up. But he really does like you."

"Well, I guess I'll have to keep playing his buddy, then."

"That way you get more info out of him, right?"

"That's correct. Thanks to Enzo being so foolish, we now know that Bruce holds the keys, and to get out of these cells, we'll obviously need those."

Her face brightened with hope. It was the happiest I had seen her yet. I was sure that wherever her parents were, they missed that face. It hurt just to think about it. I didn't have a daughter of my own, but I did know what it felt like to miss a loved one. I knew very well.

I had not been in this place for long, but I felt like I was making progress. I knew I would need to be optimistic if I wanted to get out of this cell, but what I didn't know was when I could make my next move. For now, I'd sit back on my paper-thin mattress and read *Lord of the Flies*. I'd be on an island with Ralph and Piggy instead of being locked in this cell—well, for a little while, anyway. Then, when dinnertime came around, I'd see what else I could squeeze out of Enzo.

After an hour or so of reading, I gave my eyes a rest. I looked at the only door in the room: the way out. It occurred to me that these people had probably been doing whatever it was they were doing to us for some time. I thought about how many people had been abused and killed in this place, and if I couldn't get out of here to expose these people, then what? A deluge of endless possibilities rushed into my mind. They bounced around in my head until the thoughts blended together, creating a type of head-splitting ache that left me rubbing my temples with my thumbs to mitigate some of the pain. I told myself to let it all go, to think of anything else. I needed to do this before getting back to my book.

Then, to my left, I noticed Ronnie had woken up. He sat upright and stretched, moaning when the pain in his side flared up.

"You okay, Ronnie?" Milly asked.

"I'll feel better when Jonah gets us outta here, sweetheart," Ronnie said through gritted teeth.

"Yeah, me, too," she said.

So much for not thinking about it, I thought, then said, "I wish I had a faster way to get us out of here, guys, but until I can—"

The door opened, and this time it was Bruce. He walked up to my cell with a crooked grin, which happened to match his crooked teeth. He stroked his beard a few times before saying, "You must be special, string bean, because the doc wants to see you already."

I felt a ping of unease in the pit of my stomach. I understood that it wasn't exactly normal for someone here to be taken back so soon. Hell, Milly'd been here for a week and had just now seen the doctor.

"She wants to see me already?" I asked, hoping I had heard him incorrectly.

His forehead wrinkled as he glowered at me. "You're not seriously asking me that, are you?"

At the thought of taking another beating, I decided to play it safe. "No, sir. I'm ready to go now."

"That's better. I detest when you patients don't listen to me the first time."

Patients, I thought. *That's almost funny.*

Bruce dug the keys out of his front pocket and unlocked my cell. He instructed me to turn around and place my hands on the back of my head. It felt like I was in prison, being transported to the infirmary. I felt like a prisoner, not a patient. I soon heard a couple of clicking sounds and felt cold steel being secured around my wrists as he handcuffed me. Unlike Enzo, Bruce seemed to be at least a little worried about me causing trouble.

Bruce pulled me out of the cell, his huge hands guiding and pushing me. He held the back of my neck with one hand and opened the door with the other. I felt Milly's and Ronnie's eyes watching me as I walked out of the room, but I didn't glance back at them. I had other things to focus on.

When I exited the room, I noticed another door to my left. It was only a few feet away from the room that housed our cells. A hallway leading to another room was straight ahead, but before I could get a good look to my right, Bruce shoved me forward. I walked perhaps thirty feet or so before coming to the door. I saw an intersecting hallway off to the left, but I never went down it, as Bruce opened the door and ushered me into the White Room.

As soon as I passed the door's threshold, I understood why Ronnie called the place the White Room—the walls, counters, cabinets, ceiling, floors, doors, and even the light switches were bright white. The room smelled of bleach and some other chemical I couldn't figure out, but it was pungent and made me slightly lightheaded. There were two tables off to the left. One was an examination table that you would find in any hospital, but the other appeared to be an operation table. Not only were there several surgical utensils laid out on a stainless-steel table, but the table was also surrounded by a few different machines that I didn't recognize, other than the IV stand. On the countertops were many apothecary jars filled with different medical supplies, and out of the corner of my eye, I saw another door in the far-right corner of the room.

Bruce walked me over to the examination table, and I felt somewhat calmer after not being placed on the table used for surgery. He patted the examination table and said, "Sit down." After I did, he stood next to me, silently waiting for the doctor.

I asked, "When will the doctor be in?"

"Shut up," he said. "She'll be here when she gets here."

I felt that the last part didn't clarify anything, but I kept my mouth shut.

After a few minutes passed, a lady wearing a white lab coat came strutting through the door. She had dark-blond hair that was tied back in a bun, a smooth tan complexion, a stethoscope around her neck, and a smile on her face. I thought she seemed a bit out of place here.

She pulled up a rolling chair, opened her laptop, and introduced herself as if I were a new patient getting a checkup. "Hi there. I'm Dr. Truex. Do you know why you're here, Jonah?"

"Actually, no. I have no clue why I'm here."

"You're here because you're sick. You have a very uncommon disease, and I'm here to find the cure, so to speak."

"Oh," I said with sarcasm. "So that's why Bruce and Enzo kidnapped me. It all makes sense now."

I felt a jolt of pain flare along the side of my face as Bruce backhanded me. He had zero tolerance for sarcasm, and I had forgotten that.

"That's enough, Bruce," she said. "Now, if you're ready to take this seriously, we can begin with a few questions."

I nodded.

She asked me my age, height, and weight. She asked if I was allergic to anything and then asked a few other general questions. She didn't weigh me on a scale or check my height, though. It was apparent that either my word was good enough or it simply didn't matter all that much.

Dr. Truex grabbed my wrist and checked my pulse while looking at her watch. When she finished checking my vitals, she met my eyes and asked, "Have you ever gone under general anesthesia before, Jonah?"

"No, I haven't. I've never had surgery before."

"I see. Well, I don't want to alarm you, but with the condition you have, surgery may be needed. Actually, it will most likely be needed." She tilted her head and smiled at me as if to say, *I know it sounds scary, but you need it, and I'll be gentle.*

"Do I have a choice?" I asked, knowing that I didn't.

She leaned toward me, placing one of her hands on my thigh. The smile she'd previously worn on her face had vanished, and in its place was an annoyed frown. "Jonah, I know you haven't been with us long, but I'm sure you're well acquainted with Ronnie by now, right?"

"Yes, he's a nice guy," I said, unsure where she was going with this.

"Well, Ronnie was very close to dying when he first arrived here. He didn't know it, but I can assure you that he was. Because of me and my staff, Ronnie is still alive. Next, I'll be working on his cough. He seems to have developed some sort of lung infection that I haven't been able to address just yet. I'm a very busy woman, Jonah, so please don't waste my time with stupid questions."

"Sorry, ma'am."

The smile was on her face once more. Behind that smile wasn't happiness, though. I didn't have telepathy like Milly, but I could sense the malice behind the facade.

She began typing away on her laptop for a minute or two. Bruce just stood next to me, his thumbs in his front pockets. I wondered if anyone who'd had to sit here and listen to her blatantly lie about her made-up disease actually believed her.

When Dr. Truex finished typing on her laptop, she placed her stethoscope underneath my shirt, on the bare skin of my chest. "Take several deep breaths in and out," she told me.

After I inhaled deeply the first time, I smelled something oddly familiar. A fragrant smell that I distinctly remembered smelling right before I passed out on the side of the road.

Coconuts.

Chapter 12

I waited for everything to go black. Seconds went by, but I was still conscious. I still smelled coconuts and immediately thought of the goth girl I had met on the side of the road. She'd had black hair and pale, pasty skin, and the lady before me was tan with dark-blond hair, but they smelled the same. I looked at her and tried to picture what she might look like with paler skin and a black wig. The image I created in my mind was staggering. From her cheekbones all the way down to the dimple in her chin, it was her. She was the goth girl lying on the shoulder of the road. I already knew she wasn't here to fix any of us, but now I had to figure out why we were here. I needed to—

I heard my name being called from far away, as if it were being shouted at the end of a tunnel. When I regained my focus, I realized it was Dr. Truex calling my name.

"Jonah, are you okay?"

"Yeah," I said. "I'm sorry. I spaced out."

"I'd say. Is this something that happens often?"

"No, not often."

"It may be your condition getting worse. No need to fret, though. I'm plenty capable of finding a cure. I'll fix you," she said, winking.

What I wanted to say wouldn't be good for my well-being, so I decided to be silent and just shake my head in approval.

She continued my exam by checking my blood pressure and my reflexes, and then she began wiping the crevice of my arm with an alcohol

71

wipe. "I'm going to need a blood sample, Jonah. I hope you aren't afraid of needles."

"I'm not a fan of them, but I think I'll be okay."

"Good," she said, grabbing my arm with one hand. "You may feel a little sting."

I felt the needle penetrate my skin and was glad to see she hit my vein on the first try. She took a little over one pint of my blood and handed me a small can of soda after she pulled the needle out. It was the strangest doctor's visit I'd experienced thus far in my short life. I had to find a way out of this place—and soon—before I was forced back in here so she could "fix me."

I wasn't much of a soda drinker, but I sipped on it while she typed on her laptop for a couple minutes, humming a song. It sounded like *Faith* by George Michael.

Not long after her humming, she spun around in her chair and met my eyes once more. "Well, Jonah, it was a pleasure to meet you. I'll see you again as soon as I can. As you've probably figured out already, I don't make appointments. I just don't operate that way. When I get caught up with some of the other patients, I'll have Bruce or Enzo bring you in. I should have the proper course of action for your particular disease by then. I'll perform whatever surgery needs to be done, and I must warn you that it may be invasive." She smiled after telling me that last part, like it would make her happy to cut me open and shove her gloved hand in my abdominal cavity.

"Yes, Doctor. Whatever you think needs to be done," I said, scared to say the wrong thing. I kept the possibility of a beatdown from Bruce, the bearded brute, in the back of my mind, but not so far back that I'd forget to watch what I said.

"Very good, Jonah. I'll see you soon enough. Bruce, you may lead Mr. Bosworth back to his living quarters."

"Yes, Dr. Truex," Bruce said, and then he grabbed my cuffed wrist and lifted me to my feet in a single tug.

As I was being thrust up and pushed toward the door, I wondered how she knew my full name. Then it occurred to me that she had taken my wallet with my license in it. She not only knew my name, but she had my address, as well.

Just great.

Bruce walked me back through the door. I looked all around the hall again, keeping my head straight while my eyes shifted in their sockets, moving left and right, but I found nothing more than I had the first time. I studied the area around the room we were being locked in—it wasn't much.

The only important thing I'd learned was that Dr. Truex wasn't just the doctor here; she was also the bait out there.

Bruce opened the door and shoved me back in my cell. After locking me in, he put the keys in his pocket, tugged on the cell door to make sure that it was locked, and left the room without saying anything. I glanced over at Milly and Ronnie in their cells. They were looking at me as if I were missing an arm or something.

"I'm okay, guys. Just a little tired," I said. "They took some of my blood."

"Ain't no one I know here ever been back there on the first day," Ronnie said.

Milly sat on her cot, her arms wrapped around her knees. Her eyes were half-lidded as she said, "We were worried you wouldn't be back."

"Well, I'm back. No need to worry now. She just basically gave me her version of an exam. Also, that doctor is the woman who baited me on the side of the road."

"What do you mean?" Ronnie asked.

"Ronnie, the lady you saw on the side of the road had a pale complexion and black hair, right?"

"Yeah, sure did. She seemed like one of them rock-music types."

"Right. Well, try to picture her face without the makeup. Picture her with tan skin and dark-blond hair."

Ronnie looked at the concrete floor for a few seconds. When he looked back up, his eyes were wide with insight. "Holy cow, Jonah. You ain't kiddin'. That's her. That lady is the doctor."

"Exactly. And I'm sure she told both of you that she is here to fix you. I'm right about that, aren't I?"

Milly and Ronnie both nodded in assent.

"She told me the same thing. Except she's not here to fix any of us. That much is obvious to me," I said. "This doctor is experimenting on us for some other reason. As of right now, I'm not sure why, but monetary gain would be my best guess."

"You think she's sellin' our innards to folks?" Ronnie asked.

I hadn't thought of that, but it seemed probable with what we knew. Ronnie might not sound too bright with the way he talked, but he was no dummy.

"Actually, Ronnie, there's a good possibility that's what she's doing. That would explain why Enzo says the money here is good," I said.

"Yep, and they prob'ly sellin' that blood they took from us, too."

"I wouldn't doubt it."

"Did you learn anything useful? You know, as far as getting us out of here?" Milly asked, still fighting sleep.

"Not as much as I would have liked to."

"Did you see that door to the left when you went out of the room?" she asked.

"I did."

"What do you think could be in there?"

"No clue. Maybe an exit, if we're lucky."

"What do we do now?"

"We wait for them to turn the lights out. Then we see if my plan works."

Chapter 13

Milly napped until dinnertime. Enzo dropped off the same meal we'd had for breakfast and lunch. I tried to get him to talk about anything I could, but he seemed to be too busy texting someone on his phone. It was clear I wasn't going to get any more information out of him today.

When Enzo left, we ate our dinner quietly. Having my blood taken from me earlier had made me hungry, so when I saw that Ronnie hadn't touched his apple, I traded half of my water for the piece of fruit. I was still hungry afterward, but I'd have to wait until morning, when Enzo brought out our next meal. To take my mind off my insatiable appetite, I opened my book up and read.

There wasn't a warning when they decided to turn the lights out. One second, I was reading, and the next it was pitch black. I set the book down on the concrete floor next to my cot. I tried to be as quiet as possible when I got up and took my first step toward the toilet. My arms were stretched out in front of me, and after three slow strides, I felt something cool and smooth touch the tips of my fingers.

I began to urinate into the toilet's bowl as I stuck my hand in the back of the toilet's tank, feeling around for the fill valve. I did this for two reasons: I really did have to urinate, and I thought it would be a good cover just in case the cameras had night vision.

When I found the fill valve, I adjusted the float as high as it could go. This would make the water run continuously until it was fixed or readjusted. Then, to ensure that the toilet wouldn't work at all, I reached in and broke the chain going to the flush valve, making it impossible to flush. My plan was now in motion. I just had to hope Bruce and Enzo couldn't fix it themselves. All that was left to do now was go to bed and wait.

I slept all night until the lights came back on. Before opening my eyes, I really thought for a second that I was home in my own bed, but that happy thought was gone as soon as I heard Enzo coming in with our breakfast.

"Mornin', everyone. It's breakfast time. You sleep okay, farmer Ron?" he said, laughing.

Ronnie ignored him.

Next to me, I heard the toilet water still running. The urine that remained in the toilet's bowl from last night had become acrid. I sat up in my bed and thought about what I would say to him. I didn't have long to think, though, because he was already heading my way.

"Hey, Jonah, hope you're hungry," Enzo said.

"I am, but I got to show you something."

"Show me what?"

"I used the toilet last night before bed, but it wouldn't flush. And I don't know if you can hear it or not, but the water in the tank just keeps running nonstop."

"Damn, I do hear it running now that you mention it. I'll have Bruce check it out."

"You think he can fix it?"

"I don't know. He's fixed some of the stuff around here."

Now I began to worry even more that he'd fix it. This plan had to work. There wasn't really anything else in my cell to break. "Oh, okay. Well, if he isn't able to, I'm sure I could figure it out. I've worked as a handyman for a little over a year now."

"You wanna look at it real quick and see what you think it is?"

"Sure," I said, then got up and looked in the back of the tank. I knew what was wrong, of course, but I waited ten seconds or so before telling him the reason why it wasn't working. "It looks like the fill valve has malfunctioned. The chain is broken, too. It's an easy fix, really. I could do it with some new parts and a few basic tools."

"Hmm, I better still have Bruce check it out."

"Scared you'll get in trouble?"

Enzo crossed his arms and scowled at me. "What you tryin' to say, vato?"

"Just that—"

"You think I'm scared of Bruce? I'm not scared of nobody. You hear me? You say somethin' like that again, and I'll drown you in that toilet."

I then realized I had to be careful with what I said, and how I said it, to Enzo. I thought he was developing somewhat of a soft spot for me, but it was clear that he could change his mind in a matter of seconds. I chose my next words carefully. "Sorry. I really didn't mean it like that."

"Yeah, you sure you didn't? Because it sure sounded that way to me."

"I'm sorry. That wasn't my intention. Honest."

"Uh huh," Enzo said, turning his back to me. He stormed out of the room, slamming the door.

I let out a deep breath.

Ronnie said, "Dang, Jonah, you gotta watch that one. Enzo ain't right upstairs. Some days, he's all right. Other days, he's meaner than a snake that ain't ate in a month."

"Yeah, I see that."

"Do you think Bruce will fix it, Jonah?" Milly asked.

"I don't know," I said.

An hour later, Bruce came in. He walked up to my cell and looked at me, then the toilet. "Move to the corner of the cell, put your hands on the back of your head, interlock your fingers, and don't move a muscle. If you move, you'll regret it."

"I understand," I said, then did exactly as he told me.

I was looking toward Milly's cell, my hands on my head. I mouthed the words, *What's he doing?*

He's just looking in the tank, she mouthed back.

After a minute, Bruce said, "Well, I know how to fix the chain—that's easy—but I'm not too sure about this valve here."

"It's the fill valve...sir." I thought adding that last part might help me not sound like a know-it-all.

"String bean, I think you might be right. Enzo mentioned that you said you're a handyman. Is that true?"

"Yes, sir, it is."

"Well, you think you can fix this?"

"Yes, sir."

"Well, aren't you just a respectful little string bean now that we're friends. Tell you what, if you able to fix this, I might just have another job for you."

"What job would that be?"

"Now, let's not get ahead of ourselves. First, we'll see if you're really the handyman you say you are. Now, what tools will you need?"

I told Bruce what I would need to perform the task. Then I said, "I think we really need a new fill valve. Can you or Enzo go pick one up? For now, I can just rig the chain up to make the toilet flush."

"I'll have Enzo go get one. I'll be back later today with the tools and the part. And, Jonah?"

"Yes, sir?"

He smiled. "You better not be lying."

Chapter 14

I knew I could fix the toilet, but if for some reason it went awry, I knew Bruce would turn my head into his personal punching bag. I sat on my cot, wondering about the job Bruce might have me do if this went well. I hoped it was something I was capable of doing.

Then my thoughts shifted over to my brother and Zane. I began to wonder what they were up to. I wondered if they realized I was missing or if they thought I was maybe on the run from the law. I had only been in this place for a little over twenty-four hours, and I was already missing those two. They were all I had, really. After my mom passed, I didn't have many relationships with girls in high school. Not that any of them were that interested in me, anyway. Corey was the one the girls preferred.

My dad crossed my mind shortly after. I figured he probably thought I was in jail and was too stubborn to call him to get bailed out. He was still very disappointed in me—that much, I was sure of.

I closed my eyes and let out a deep, slow breath. In the vast darkness of my mind, I pictured the hallway outside of this room. I had to find out what was behind that first door to the left. Maybe it was an exit; maybe it wasn't. Either way, I tried to think of ways to get through the mystery door. Then I remembered the hallway to the right. I wondered where it led to.

I was so eager to leave this room and find a way out, but I couldn't with the little bit of information I'd gathered. I knew I had to get out of here as soon as possible, because if I didn't, one of two things was apt to happen: I'd either go absolutely crazy or I'd die. I wasn't ready to die yet, so my only option was to focus on getting out of here. I ran several escape plans in my head over and over until it began to ache. When I deduced that none of them were viable, I went back to reading my novel until Bruce or Enzo came in with lunch or the parts for the toilet.

It just so happened to be both. Around noon, each of them came in. Enzo held a tray with our food, and Bruce held a plastic bag in one hand, along with the few tools I'd requested in the other. Enzo handed us our meals in silence. His eyes were cast down, looking at the food he slid into our cells.

Bruce, on the other hand, was smiling. He handed me the bag with the new fill valve in it, then the tools. "All right, string bean. Let's see if you're pulling my leg or not."

Being as nervous as I was, food didn't really appeal to me, so I left it on the paper plate on the floor and began the process of changing the fill valve. First, I needed the water turned off, or else water would just keep spewing out when I separated the water line from the bottom of the fill valve.

"I'll need the water turned off for a few minutes, sir," I said to Bruce.

"Sure," he said, and then he turned to his colleague. "Enzo, go turn the water off at the well for me."

"Why can't you do it?" Enzo asked.

"Because I asked you to do it."

Enzo scoffed and left the room, leaving the door open.

I paid attention to two things as Enzo walked out: the way he was getting annoyed with Bruce and which way he went when he left the room. Bruce told him to shut the water off at the well, and of course the well would be outside. Enzo made a sharp left as he exited. It was then that I knew where that door to the left led to: outside.

I placed the tools and the new fill valve on the concrete floor next to the toilet and waited for Enzo to return. A few minutes later, I heard a door close. Then Enzo came back into the room.

"We good to go?" Bruce asked Enzo.

Enzo nodded.

Bruce looked back to me. "Okay, have at it."

Bruce and Enzo watched as I grabbed the pliers, got down on a knee, and began to work. I took my time, carefully loosening and tightening the plastic nuts on the water line and valve. I didn't want to chance making a mistake or breaking anything. After a short period of time, I had the new valve installed and the chain going to the flapper fixed.

"Okay, it should work now," I said. "You can turn the water back on."

"You heard the man, Enzo," Bruce said, not turning to look at him.

A scowl appeared on Enzo's face, but he didn't say anything. He cast a brief glance at Bruce and then exited the room.

After a minute or two, I heard the water come on and begin to fill the tank. I bent over the toilet and watched as the valve did its job.

Around the time the tank was full of water, Enzo stood at the door's threshold but chose not to come in. "It's on," he said, then walked down the hallway.

Bruce said, "Well, we already knew that, didn't we, string bean? Go ahead. Give 'er a flush."

I flushed the toilet, and everything functioned as it was supposed to. I turned to Bruce and said, "Need anything else fixed? I know I'm young, but I've got over a year's experience fixing various things."

"Now why would you want to help us?"

"It passes the time. And I figure it'll give me some brownie points, if I'm going to be honest."

"I'm sure Dr. Truex will be pleased to know she has a patient capable of fixing some of the issues around here. I'm just glad I didn't have to tinker with it for an hour or so. You're all right, string bean."

Bruce's eyes shifted to Milly's cell. She was sitting quietly, listening to our conversation. "Hey there. You want to see the doctor again?" Bruce asked Milly.

"No. Please don't make me," she pleaded.

"Easy now, girl. Don't you worry. Farmer Ron over there is next on the list for an appointment, anyway."

"For what?" Ronnie asked.

"For whatever she has to do to you. Now shut it," Bruce said, his voice getting louder.

Ronnie didn't make a sound. None of us did.

Bruce continued to stare at Ronnie. Finally, he said, "Look, farmer Ron, I know you're still in some pain from your last surgery, but don't you fret. The doctor has a remedy just for you."

Milly glanced at me then. Her eyes were wide, and a single tear began to trickle down her cheek. I saw something else in her eyes: knowledge. She'd read Bruce's mind as he'd looked at Ronnie just then. She knew what was going to happen to him.

Bruce chuckled after toying with Ronnie and left the room.

Milly began to cry harder as soon as the door closed behind Bruce.

"What's wrong, sweetheart?" Ronnie asked.

"They...they..." She was having trouble getting the words out.

"They what?"

"They are going to...kill you," she said, the tears now streaming down her face.

Ronnie looked at the concrete floor in front of him. He seemed to be lost in deep thought. A minute later, Milly's crying subsided.

"It's okay, sweetheart," Ronnie said.

"No. It's not okay. You don't deserve to die. I don't want you to go," she said.

"It's outta our hands, Milly. I ain't gettin' any better as it—" Ronnie began to cough again. This time, specks of blood came out of his mouth and hit the concrete floor.

I wanted to help him so badly, but there was nothing I could do. I was stuck in a cell without enough information or a viable plan to get us out of here.

Ronnie stopped coughing and wiped the blood from his lips with the back of his hand. "Milly, jus' because I ain't gon' make it don't mean you are gon' to give up on gettin' outta here. Promise me that."

"I promise, Ronnie," she said. "You were my only friend in here until Jonah got here, you know?"

"I know it, sweetheart. You were mine, too. I believe Jonah's gon' be true to his word, though. I ain't known him that long, but you can tell he's a special guy. And, honey, you're a special girl. Very special, actually. If anyone's ever gettin' outta this damn place, it's you two."

Ronnie began to cough up small amounts of blood again as soon as he finished speaking. Milly and I recognized that Ronnie was going to die soon either way. His condition just kept getting worse, and the doctor here wasn't interested in making him any better.

"Ronnie, maybe—" Milly said, but she stopped when she saw the door begin to open.

It was Enzo, and Dr. Truex was with him. Enzo held a tray with only two plates on it. Dr. Truex came in holding a syringe with a clear substance in her right hand. She didn't even attempt to hide it. Enzo put the plates in front of our cells, but we didn't move. The thought of food made me feel nauseated knowing what I knew. Milly shifted her eyes toward Ronnie, and he glanced back and forth between Milly, me, and Dr. Truex. He looked like a wounded animal caught in a trap.

Enzo waited for us to grab our plates. When we didn't, he asked, "What's wrong? You guys not hungry or somethin'?"

"We both have a stomachache," I said.

Dr. Truex looked at me as if she knew I was lying, then said, "Hmm, perhaps I should get you both in to make sure it's nothing serious."

"No!" Milly shouted, then clapped her hand over her mouth.

I tried not to look as surprised as I was. "It's not that bad of a stomachache."

"I see," Dr. Truex said. "I'm glad to hear that, because I need to get Ronnie in immediately to see if we can stop that cough once and for all."

"And how you plannin' on doin' that?" Ronnie asked.

"That's classified, you dummy," Enzo said.

"No need to be so rude, Enzo," Dr. Truex said, then rested her eyes on Ronnie. "I promise to explain everything there is to know about this operation as soon as we get you into my office. Now, we mustn't waste much more time, I'm afraid."

Bruce walked into the room again. He held the keys to our cell doors in his right hand and headed toward Ronnie's cell. "Okay, farmer Ron, you've been here long enough. You know the drill."

Ronnie had difficulty attempting to stand up, so he lay face down on his mattress instead. He faced us with his hands behind his back, and I wished he hadn't. It would have been a little easier on Milly if he had been looking the other way. We watched Bruce open the door and handcuff Ronnie. Enzo held him down, and Dr. Truex entered the cell last.

"What's goin' on? Why all three of y'all in here?" Ronnie asked, weak and scared.

"Shhh, you're going to feel a little pinch," the doctor told him.

"Wait," I said. "How are you going to explain everything to him if you sedate him?"

"Now isn't the time for questions, Mr. Bosworth," Dr. Truex said, then jabbed the syringe into Ronnie's neck.

Ronnie yelped, and his eyelids slowly began to close. Shortly after, his body went limp. Milly suppressed a scream and put her hands over her eyes.

I continued to watch and tried to keep my breathing controlled. My heart was racing, my nerves were shot, and I just wanted all of this to be over. I felt like giving up. I felt like I was fighting a battle I'd never win.

Bruce flipped Ronnie over and grabbed him by his wrists. He told Enzo to grab Ronnie's ankles, and then they exited the cell and carried Ronnie out of the room.

It would be the last time Milly and I ever saw him.

Chapter 15

Our food sat outside of our cells. Milly sat on her cot, her arms wrapped around her legs, crying for a couple hours. I stared at the door Ronnie had been carried through, trying to understand why we were here and why these people were experimenting on us. I had a few ideas, but I was certain about none of them. And not knowing was driving me mad. I tried opening my book to escape, but it was no use. I couldn't stop thinking about Ronnie. Finally, around eight-thirty, Milly stopped crying and fell asleep. The lights in the room were still on, but in another thirty minutes they would turn them off on us.

I picked my book up again to try to read a little before bed, but as I opened the paperback, Dr. Truex came into the room. She saw that Milly was sleeping and tried not to wake her. The sleeves of the doctor's white lab coat were stained red with what appeared to be blood. It looked fresh and wet.

"Jonah," she said, "I hate to have to tell you this, but Ronnie is no longer with us. I tried my absolute best, but with the rare disease he had, I just couldn't save him."

I was biting my tongue hard enough to leave indentations in it. I felt a single tear trickle down my cheek. I tried to trick myself by imagining they'd bring him back alive and well, but I knew they wouldn't. I knew he had been here for a while now and that they no longer needed him. They got what they wanted from Ronnie, and now that he was no longer useful to them, they'd disposed of him.

"Jonah?" she asked me. "Are you okay?"

I wasn't sure why she was acting like she cared or why she would go through the trouble of pretending just to gain my trust. I couldn't say what I wanted to. I had to hold back my anger and—

"Stop acting like you care," Milly cried from her bed, now awake. "You don't give a crap about us. I am sick of this place. I want my mom and my dad!"

Dr. Truex gave her a startled glance. "Well, don't you have a mouth on you. You're in this place because you need help, and I'm the only doctor in this country who can give you the help you need, you brat. That's why you were sent to me."

Milly was out of bed, shaking with fury, her hands wrapped around the cell's steel bars, glaring at the doctor. I was worried for her well-being more than ever.

Through clenched teeth, Milly said, "You're a liar."

"And you're not very well behaved," Dr. Truex said.

"I know what you're really up to now. Your thoughts just told me."

"Oh, we have a mind reader here. How adorable. Let's hear what my thoughts told you, Milly."

"That you're not really—"

"Milly, stop!" I said. "He's gone. I know it hurts."

"But she's ly—"

"Milly. *Think*," I said, pausing for a few moments so she could read my thoughts. *I know she's lying, but we have to keep your ability a secret. We'll need it to get us out of here.* "Dr. Truex tried her best. I'm sure she didn't want to lose Ronnie to this disease, either."

"That's correct, Jonah," Dr. Truex said. "And believe me, I don't like that I have to quarantine you guys like this, but it's the only way to keep this disease from spreading to others. And before you ask, I have methods to boost my immune system—as well as my staff's—to keep from getting the disease you two have."

Milly must have read my thoughts, because she didn't say anything else to the doctor. She turned around, crying quietly, and got back on her cot.

"May I speak with you a moment?" Dr. Truex asked me.

"Sure."

"Bruce told me how quick and easily you fixed the toilet in your cell. Could I get you to take a look at a ceiling fan for me?"

"Yeah, that's no problem. I've switched out a few of those before. Nothing to it."

"Great. I'll have Bruce show it to you later if you're up to it. If you need tonight to mourn Ronnie, I'll understand."

I glanced over at Milly, who was lying still on her cot. She was facing Ronnie's cell. I wanted to stay to console her because she was taking it pretty hard, but I also needed to figure out how to get us out of here. I met the doctor's eyes and said, "I'm up to it."

"Good," she said, then left the room.

It was just Milly and me now. She continued to stare off at Ronnie's cell.

"Milly, are you okay?"

"Not really."

"Remember what Ronnie said. He wants us to get out of here. He wouldn't want us to just give up."

"I'm not giving up. I'm just so mad at that lady."

"So am I. I don't like having to pretend that I'm fine or that I'm not upset about Ronnie, because I am. I know they killed him, and that's why I'm going to fix their stupid fan and learn as much as I can—"

"Okay, string bean, let's go," Bruce said as he opened the door and began walking toward my cell to unlock it. "That fan isn't going to fix itself, and I'm sure as hell not going to fix it."

He opened the cell door and said, "Now, do I need to cuff you, or are you going to be cool?"

"I'll be cool. Not like I'm going to outmuscle you, right?"

"Right. And if you try, I'll break your ribs."

"That's fair," I said, walking out of the cell.

Bruce grabbed my arm and walked me out of the room. I looked back at Milly, but she continued facing Ronnie's cell. I felt so bad for her.

When I went through the door's threshold, Bruce led me to the first door on the left—the one Enzo had come out of earlier when he turned the water off at the well. I hoped that one way or another, this room would be the key to getting out of here.

Bruce twisted the doorknob and escorted me into the room. He flipped on a light switch, and the bulbs in the ceiling fan cast a dim light. I saw four computer monitors resting on two long tables. They were the monitors for the cameras in our cells. On the screens, I saw all five cells as well as Milly still lying on her cot. She hadn't moved. The wires to the monitors were scattered all over the ground. I surmised that that was Bruce and Enzo's handywork, but nonetheless the cameras were functioning. As Milly had told me, they didn't pick up sound. That, or they didn't have any speakers wired in.

Bruce saw me eyeing the monitors and smacked me hard upside the head. "String bean, we may be friends now, but you need to keep your head on straight. That means you pay attention to the task at hand. You understand me?"

My face scrunched up as I looked down at the floor, blinking several times. The pain from the strike made my eyes water, but I refused to let a tear fall from them. Still looking down, I said, "Yes."

"Yes what?" Bruce said, squeezing my bicep with his enormous hand.

"I understand."

"Good. Next time, I won't be so gentle."

If he was being gentle just then, I'd be unconscious from the next strike to the head. I put my hand up to my face and felt the warm spot that had just been smacked. Meeting Bruce's eyes, I asked, "Do you have a step stool I could use?"

"Just use a chair," Bruce said, pointing toward a folded-up steel chair that was leaning against the wall on the other side of the room.

I walked over, keeping my head straight while looking all around with my eyes. I saw a door but didn't see any light coming from underneath it, and I couldn't be sure if it led outside or to another room. All I knew was that Enzo somehow got to the well outside from this room. When I reached the chair, I picked it up and hauled it over to the ceiling fan. I placed the chair under the fan and instantly noticed that I would have to loosen a couple of screws.

"Do you have a screwdriver I could use to loosen these?" I asked.

Bruce placed the palm of his hand on his forehead and said, "Dammit, string bean, you should have told me you needed a screwdriver."

"I'm sorry. I didn't know I—"

"Just shut up," he said, grabbing my arm.

He put a handcuff on my right wrist, then put the other cuff around the fan blade's metal bracket. He clicked both cuffs and left me there, standing on a chair with my arm cuffed to a ceiling fan.

"I'll be right back. Don't go anywhere." He laughed. "As if you have a choice."

As soon as he closed the door, I began pushing on the cuff with my left hand. It was tight, and the metal dug into my skin. The metal on bone hurt like hell, and my head still tingled somewhat from being smacked, but I had to get out of here. After ten seconds or so, the cuff slid off and I stepped quietly down from the chair. I had no idea how long Bruce would be, and not knowing made my heart pound madly inside my chest. I darted over to the door where the chair had been propped up against the wall, and I was thrilled when I saw that it was unlocked.

I entered the room and saw what seemed to be a living room, although it didn't have a single window except for one on the door. It was still odd to see such a room in a place like this. On the other side of the room was the door with the small, tinted window roughly the size of a football. The door was gray, was made from steel, and had three different locking mechanisms. I rushed over to it and peeked through the small window, discovering that it did in fact lead outside. I quickly twisted the doorknob, and to my surprise the knob twisted around as if it were going to open the door. However, with the locks securing it, the door didn't budge. I'd thought, just for a second, that I was on my way out of here. Breaking the window wasn't an option, because even though I was skinny, I wouldn't fit through the small opening.

I began to examine the locks. Two of them were deadbolts that would require keys, and the top one was just a steel rod that locked into a hole in the doorframe. I was certain I would need the keys Bruce had to get out of here, but I knew he wouldn't be looking for that screwdriver forever.

I started walking back but stopped when I saw an open laptop on a small rolltop desk in the corner of the room. The screen displayed what seemed to be an email inbox. It was like nothing I had ever seen before. On the screen was an email Dr. Truex had sent to someone with the name Thomas O. In the message, she informed him that she had several organs ready for purchase and that they would discuss the price in person.

Suddenly, my face felt hot, as if I were running a fever. I had speculated that this place must be selling body parts to organ traffickers, but now that my suspicions were substantiated by the email, this whole situation felt much more real. I knew for sure that I would die here if I didn't get out soon.

I heard a noise close by that sounded like someone dropping something. I prayed that Bruce wasn't in the other room waiting for me to come back in. I was hesitant to peek back in the room, but I couldn't afford to waste any more time—just in case Bruce hadn't made it back yet. When I saw that the room appeared to be empty, I hurried over to the chair and began working my left wrist through the cuff. I almost had it on when I remembered that the manacle was originally on my right. I pulled it out and started twisting my right hand through the metal cuff.

It was much more difficult putting it back on, and I was starting to doubt that I would even get it around my wrist with the cuff giving me so much trouble.

Then I heard heavy footfalls coming from outside of the room.

Bruce was close.

With increasing trepidation, I spat on my right hand to lubricate the cuff and began pulling down on it as hard as I could. I gritted my teeth and kept constant pressure on the manacle, spinning it as I pulled it down. I saw the doorknob turning, and as the door began to open, the cuff slid back over my hand. It was around my wrist, and Bruce was closing the door behind him. I wiped the saliva from my hand while he was turned around, and I prayed that my skin wouldn't turn too red from forcing the cuff back on.

Bruce looked me up and down for a moment, and I held my breath as he did. "Hey, string bean, this screwdriver better do it, because it's the only one I could find."

"Looks like it should work," I said.

"Good," Bruce said, then dug in his pocket, pulled out the keys, and unlocked the cuff from the fan.

He pulled me down from the chair by the cuff still connected to my wrist, and I landed flat on my back as I hit the floor. It knocked most of the wind out of me.

"Whoops, just couldn't help myself," he said, laughing.

I lay on my back, trying to fill my lungs with air as he chuckled to himself.

He glanced down at me and said, "Okay, get up. You still have to get this fan figured out before bed. Let me see your arm so I can take this cuff off." I gave him my arm, and he stared at it for a moment. "You've got some sensitive skin, don't you?" he asked, still looking at the redness around my hand.

"Yes, sir," I said. "It doesn't take much."

"Ah, I see. You have little Nancy-boy skin," he said, smirking. "Hurry up. I got other shit to do tonight that doesn't involve watching you fix a ceiling fan."

I got up, taking in deep breaths as I did. I stood on the chair again and stuck my hand out at him with my palm open.

Bruce looked at my hand, then back at me. "What the hell do you want, string bean? A high five?"

"No, sir. I need the screwdriver."

"Oh, right. Here," he said, handing me the tool.

I grabbed ahold of the screwdriver's handle and went to take it, but he didn't let go. He furrowed his brow and said, "Now don't get any stupid ideas. If you try to stab me, I won't hesitate to shoot you with this." Bruce lifted his shirt to reveal the 9mm pistol in the waistband of his denim jeans. "Do we have an understanding?"

I looked at the gun. It was large and silver in color. *If only I could take that from him without getting myself killed*, I thought. "Yes. You have made yourself clear."

"Okay, good. Now get this fixed already," he said, releasing the screwdriver.

I took it and stepped back on the chair. I reached up and loosened the screws on the fan, removing the cover so I could access the wires. As I figured, there wasn't anything wrong with the wiring. The fan was just bad.

"You're going to need to get a whole new ceiling fan, sir," I said.

"Great. That just adds to the list of crap I already have to do tonight. Thanks a lot, kid."

"I'm sorry. This fan looks like it's been here a long time."

"Well, Sherlock, that's because it has. Now give me that screwdriver and get your scrawny ass down here. I need to get you back to your cell before lights out. Like I said, I have shit to do."

I gave him the screwdriver and began to get down, but the chair I was standing on slid out from under me. I tried to catch myself but landed on my back again. This time, the wind was completely knocked out of me. I tried to suck in as much air as I could, but my lungs just wouldn't function. For a few seconds, I panicked, wondering if I would ever breathe again. Soon after that harrowing thought, though, my lungs gradually began to work.

Looking at him from the floor, I asked, "Why'd you do that?"

"Do what?" Bruce asked, smiling.

"Kick the chair out from under me?"

"Because it's funny and I can do whatever the hell I want. That a good enough reason for you, string bean?" He grabbed me by the shirt and lifted me to my feet. "Walk," he said, then pushed me forward.

At that moment, I wanted nothing more than to turn around and knee him in the groin, but I knew I couldn't take him. He was too big, too strong, and he had a gun in arm's reach.

Bruce led me out of the room and back to the one that housed our cells. Milly was still on her cot, presumably sleeping. The lights were on but wouldn't be for much longer according to the clock on the wall.

Bruce pushed me into my cell, I fell on my cot, and he locked the door. "Sleep tight, string bean. I'll pick up that new ceiling fan either tonight or tomorrow. We'll see how tonight goes first."

He chuckled to himself as he walked away. I was glad to see him leave, as I had had enough of him for the day.

I rested my sore head and body on the cot and looked up at the dusty ceiling. I wondered how in the hell I'd get those keys from Bruce. Soon, the lights went out, and all I could see was total darkness and four blinking red lights in each corner of the room.

Chapter 16

Even on my rock-hard mattress, I fell asleep within a minute. I dreamed of being taken back into the White Room by Bruce and Enzo. They each gripped one of my arms and held me down on the operation table while Dr. Truex sat nearby, next to her stainless-steel surgical utensils. I asked them what was going on, what they were going to do to me. Dr. Truex stood over my body. A blinding white light shined behind her head. She held a scalpel in her right hand as her left hand caressed my chin. She met my eyes and said, "I'm going to make you all better, of course." Then she buried the scalpel in my chest, and I woke up.

In the pitch black, lying down on my side, I was sweating all over. Now knowing Ronnie had been killed in the White Room, just the thought of that damn room made my heart race. I didn't want to go back in there ever again for fear I'd suffer the same fate as Ronnie.

My back was sore from the fall, and a sharp pain made its way down my lower back as I shifted to my other side. I suppressed the urge to yell, but a groan escaped me.

"Jonah, that you?" Milly asked.

"Sorry to wake you."

"Are you okay? Did they do something to you like they did to Ronnie?"

"No, nothing like that. I—"

"Bruce threw you on the floor or kicked a chair?"

"He kicked the chair out from under me, and I landed on my back pretty hard."

"Sorry, I normally hear people's thoughts clearly, but I'm not fully awake yet. Are you okay, though? Your back, I mean.

"Yeah, I think so. I'm a skateboarder, so falling is something I'm familiar with."

"You don't really look like a skateboarder."

"You don't really look telepathic," I said, then heard her laugh a little.

"So, how'd it go out there? Did you fix the fan or whatever? I promise not to read your thoughts this time."

"Well, the fan didn't get fixed. Bruce is going to have to pick up a new one. I did learn a lot, though."

"Like what?"

"Like how we can get out of here."

Milly was silent for several seconds. I wasn't sure if she was reading my thoughts or listening to her own.

"I promise I wasn't trying to hear your thoughts. Well, I accidentally did just then. But I was thinking to myself."

"Thinking about what?"

"Thinking about if you do find us a way out of here. What if we're in the middle of nowhere? What if they have guards or something outside of the building. They'll kill us if we get caught trying to escape."

"We have no choice, Milly. They will eventually kill us like they did Ronnie if we don't get out of here soon."

She was silent again for a few seconds, then said, "How do we get out of here?"

"Well, first we need Enzo to get ahold of Bruce's keys somehow. I'll have to persuade Enzo to obtain them one way or another. Then, the tricky part: getting them away from Enzo. I'll need something—"

"Shhh, listen," Milly whispered.

Faint voices were getting louder as they went down the hall and got closer to us. It sounded like the voices were bickering back and forth like an old married couple, which led me to believe it was Bruce and Enzo. When they got near the door, I could finally interpret what they were saying to each other.

"Just do as I say, dammit," Bruce said to Enzo.

"Man, just hurry up, would you?"

"Shut up and let me find my keys."

"This is why I need a set of my own keys, man. I've been here for two years and—"

"Found 'em. Now shut your piehole."

I heard the door unlock, the doorknob turn, and the two large men enter the room. As the hallway light flooded into the room, I shielded my eyes but was still blinded by its brightness. I kept my eyes closed for about ten seconds. I needed that time to shake off the disoriented feeling I had. When I opened my eyes again, I looked toward Milly's cell so the light wouldn't be as intense. My vision was still marginally blurry, but I could see that Bruce was opening the two cells that had been vacant since I arrived here days ago.

"Slide him in," I heard Bruce tell Enzo.

I watched as Enzo slid an unconscious body into the far cell to the right of the door. I couldn't see the person in the cell, but it appeared that Milly and I had a new roommate. When Enzo walked out of the dark cell, he grabbed another unconscious person from the concrete floor and slid that body into the other cell. Bruce held the cell door open for Enzo as he pulled the body by the ankles. This body, I could see a little better since it was closer to the door. I saw dark-blue denim jeans, a Tampa Bay Rays t-shirt, and a recognizable face that broke my heart and took my breath away at the same time. It was Corey.

Chapter 17

When I was younger, around the age of eight, I accidentally ran my brother over with my bicycle. It was summer break, and we were playing out in the yard while our mom cleaned the house. Dad was grilling hotdogs and hamburgers and peeking over at us every so often to make sure we weren't doing anything that we shouldn't be doing. Corey wore his Ninja Turtles mask and periodically jumped out at me from behind bushes and trees around the yard. He had succeeded in startling me a few times, so I quickened my pace on my Huffy to scare him. I soon found out that that was a colossal mistake, as he jumped out from behind a tree and didn't have enough time to get out of the way. My handlebars connected with his face and knocked him out. I threw the bike down and rushed over to where he lay on his back, not moving a muscle. I thought I had killed him, so I screamed. My dad rushed over to us and pulled Corey's mask off. Blood trickled from a shallow cut where the plastic mask had sliced the skin on his face from the impact. He had some bruising but woke up shortly after my dad yelled at me for hurting him.

I was so scared then—sick with fear, even—but nowhere near as scared as I was when I saw Corey being slid into that cell across from me. This was fear I had never experienced before.

I watched as Bruce locked the cell Corey was in and began to walk toward the door leading into the hall. He didn't say anything to Milly or me, and that was good because I would have said the wrong thing and been beaten senseless. When Bruce and Enzo left, the room went dark again. I groped around my cell until I found the toilet, and then I puked up what little I had in my stomach.

"Jonah, what's going on?" Milly asked, then paused for a moment before reading my mind. "Oh my God. Are you sure that's him? Your brother?"

I flushed the toilet, took a deep breath, and managed to say, "Yes, it's him." The words came out hoarse, as if I had lost my voice.

"I'm so sorry, Jonah," Milly whispered.

I couldn't say anything at that moment. My thoughts became nebulous. I tried to focus and wondered, through the haziness of my mind, how Corey could have ended up here. Bruce was supposed to be fetching me a damn ceiling fan and came back with my brother, unconscious and bleeding. I was so mad, so confused. Core shouldn't be here. Then a thought crossed my mind: *Do they know he's my brother?* They had my wallet and access to my driver's license, which had my information all over it.

I couldn't go back to sleep, not with all of this careening around in my head.

After ten minutes or so, I found my voice. It was there, but not completely. "Milly?"

"Yes, Jonah?"

"I need you to do something for me from here on out."

"No problem. What is it?"

"When Bruce, Enzo, or Dr. Truex come in here, I need you to focus as hard as you can. We have to know exactly what's on their minds."

"I try. I really do. It's just that sometimes they scare me so much that my *know-stuff* stops working. It makes it so hard to hear what they are thinking. I just get worried about what's going to happen to me when they come in here."

"I feel that fear, too, Milly, but we have to be brave. You understand? I have an idea, but I don't have all the pieces to the puzzle just yet."

"I'll try real hard, Jonah. I promise."

I stared at the cell Corey had been placed in. I couldn't see him, of course—not with the lights off—but I thought maybe he'd wake up if I called for him. "Core," I said. "Core, wake up. It's Jonah."

Nothing. But I could hear him breathing, at least.

Milly said, "Jonah, I think they gave him the same shot that made us go to sleep."

"I believe you're right. I just want him to know that I'm here and that I'm going to get us out of this place...and that I missed him."

Milly and I waited in the dark, not saying much. I couldn't go back to sleep knowing that my brother was in a cell twelve feet away from me. I wondered what my dad was thinking right now. He had probably already called the cops and reported Corey missing. I had to stop thinking about it. I could picture him sitting on the couch, sick with worry and feeling helpless. He lost my mom, and now both of his sons were missing. I had never felt so bad for my father. I told myself at that moment that if I somehow got out of here alive, I would hug my dad and not let go for quite some time.

I was staring at the ceiling when the lights came on. They were bright, and it took my eyes a few seconds to adjust. I looked over at Corey, who had started to stir in his sleep. When he finally woke up, he shielded his eyes from the room's lighting. I saw the dried blood under his nose and the rip around the collar of his shirt. It was hard to see him like that, but part of me, in a strange way, was happy to see him. I watched Corey look around in his cell. He shuffled over and sat on the cot, his hands rubbing the back side of his head.

"Hey, Core," I said softly, knowing Enzo would be in at any moment with breakfast.

He looked up. "Jonah?"

I met his eyes. His got large and round, and then his brow furrowed as his mouth hung slightly open.

"It's me, Core. Believe it."

"Where the hell are we?"

"I don't have a clue. I've been here for a few days now. How did you end up here, too?"

"We were looking for you. Zane told me what happened. When we didn't find you at the police department, we figured you were on the run. But after a day or two of you not calling me or Zane, we got worried about you. We thought you might have crashed your bike somewhere. So we went looking for you in Zane's Honda."

In the cell to the right of Corey's, the body inside got to his knees. "Corey? You here?" the man said, blinking his eyes several times in Corey's direction.

"Yeah, Zane, I'm right here," Corey said. "Guess who else is here."

"Who?" Zane asked, then turned around in his cell. When he saw me, his eyes got large and round, just like Corey's had a moment ago. You would have thought he had just seen a ghost. "Jonah, no way, man. Is this where you've—"

"Shhh," I said. "Keep your voice down. Enzo will be in any second, and we don't want them knowing that we know each other."

"Sorry," Zane said, speaking softer now.

"It's okay. We're going to be okay. Just don't trust these people. They're not here to fix us. Don't believe anything the doctor tells you guys." I took a deep breath and noticed Milly sitting upright on her cot, biting her lip in a pensive way. "Milly, you okay?"

She glanced at me with wide eyes. "They're close, Jonah."

To my right, I heard Corey say, "What doctor?"

The door opened, and Dr. Truex walked into the room, followed by Bruce and Enzo. She looked at me first, grinning. "Jonah, Milly, have you two met your new neighbors yet?"

Milly didn't say anything, but I nodded my head and said, "Yes, Dr. Truex, we have."

"Good. I hope you're all well acquainted now." Her smile faded away as she turned away from me. "I'd like to introduce myself to each of you now rather than twice later on. As Jonah has already said, my name is Dr. Truex. I am here to fix you all. You see, each of you has a rare disease that will inevitably kill you. I'm here to make sure that doesn't happen. I'll be getting blood from you both as soon as I can. I'm not going to beat around the bush. Surgery will be necessary to save your lives."

"You expect us to believe that garbage? Why would you put us in cages if you were really going to help us?" Corey asked.

"First off, that was awfully rude of you. But to answer your question, you are in these cells for your own protection, believe it or not. With the disease you all inexplicably have, you're apt to attack us or even one another at any given moment. When that happens, you won't remember it at all. But please believe me. I've seen it many times. Any more questions before I introduce you to Bruce and Enzo?"

"Yeah. Do you get all of your *patients* on the side of the road after you jump and drug them?" Corey asked, sneering at the three of them.

"Clever one, aren't you? I see you're going to be troublesome. We have a way to deal with troublesome patients, don't we, Bruce?"

"We sure do," Bruce said, grinning and cracking his hairy knuckles.

"Not even going to deny that you jumped us on the side of the road, are you?" Corey asked, laughing nervously.

"You ignorant boy, don't you understand anything? As I've mentioned, the disease you have causes severe delirium. You thought you were on the side of the road getting kidnapped, but you were actually sent here from a mental institution that could no longer keep you."

"That's bull!" Corey shouted, slamming his hands on the cell door.

Dr. Truex turned around and sighed. "Bruce, Enzo, show this troublesome boy how we deal with disobedience in my hospital."

Dr. Truex stood by the door while Bruce dug the keys out of his front pocket. As Bruce unlocked the cell, Corey stood there ready to defend himself. I watched with clenched fists as Bruce and Enzo charged into the cell, grabbing Corey and throwing him against the cell wall. Bruce picked him up off the ground and punched him in his stomach. Corey grabbed his mid-section and fell back over. He was looking at me while the side of his face rested on the cold concrete floor, struggling to get his breath back. With tears in my eyes, I mouthed the words, *Stay down. Don't fight back.* Enzo reached down and lifted Corey up to his feet by his hair.

I couldn't take it anymore. I took a deep breath and said, "Enzo, I think he's had enough. Your point has been made."

Enzo turned around, still gripping Corey's hair with a tight fist. The one crazed eye of his that I could see resembled a wild animal right before it pounced on its prey. "You better mind your own business, vato, or else I'll be in your cell next."

He returned his attention to Corey and slugged him in the stomach. Corey fell back to the ground, struggling to breathe even worse now. I bit my tongue. It was the only thing I could do to prevent myself from saying something.

"Okay, Enzo, that's enough," Dr. Truex said. "The two of you can come out of there now." She walked over to the cell, bending down to talk to Corey. "What is your name?"

Corey tried to say his name but was still working on getting his breath back.

"Tell me your name, or my friends are going to come back in there and get it for me."

Corey tried again, but nothing intelligible came out.

"Fine. Have it your way. Bruce, Enzo—"

"It's Corey!" Zane said. "His name is Corey. Please don't hurt him anymore."

"Okay, Corey, did you learn something today?" Dr. Truex asked.

Corey shook his head, suggesting that he did.

"Good. And thank you, Zane."

"How'd you know my name and not his?" Zane asked.

She curled her lips up into a smile. "Well, Zane, we have your driver's license, but Corey here didn't have any identification on him."

"Oh," Zane said.

"Now, I take it the silly questions are over with, yes?" she asked, looking around the room at all of us. "Good. Zane, since you've been so cooperative, how about you eat your breakfast and then come back with us for a blood sample. I have a few questions of my own to ask you."

"Okay," Zane said, then took the food from Enzo and began to nibble on the bread.

"When you have finished your meal, Enzo will escort you to my office. I believe that is all for now. Bruce, unlock Zane's cell and come with me. I'd like to have a discussion."

She and Bruce walked out of the room and left us with Enzo.

He gave me my meal last. As he laid my food down in front of my cell, he spat on the bread and stomped the apple. "That's for tryin' to tell me what to do. You're lucky I halfway like you, or else I would just come in there and rearrange your face. You try me again and I'll show you exactly what I mean. You feel me?"

"Yeah. I didn't mean any disrespect," I said.

"Next time you think we ain't handling somethin' right, just do yourself a favor, vato, and keep it to yourself."

"Understood, Enzo."

"Good. Here, I feel kind of bad. Let me get you a fresh apple."

Enzo ambled over to Corey's cell and grabbed Corey's apple off his tray. He rubbed the apple on his tank top as if to polish it up. "Here, Jonah. You deserve this more than that kid."

"Thanks," I said softly.

Enzo nodded and then went over to Zane's cell. "Let's go," he said to Zane, who was still eating his bread.

After seeing what they had done to Corey, Zane didn't ask for more time to eat. He set what was left of the bread down on his tray and waited for Enzo to cuff him. As Zane walked by, I saw that his eyes were watery and that he was breathing faster than normal. He looked in my direction for a brief second, and I mouthed the words, *It'll be okay.*

We all watched as Zane left with Enzo, and I hoped like hell I wouldn't be made a liar.

Chapter 18

As soon as the door closed, Milly and I shifted our eyes toward Corey, who was still lying on the floor, holding his mid-section.

"Corey, are you okay? Did they break anything?" I asked.

"No," he muttered.

"No, you're not okay? Or no, they didn't break anything?"

"Didn't break anything." He seemed to be getting his breath back. He pushed off the concrete floor, positioning himself upright, his back resting against the cot. "Are they going to kill us, Jonah?"

"If we don't get out of here sooner rather than later...yes."

"Jonah's been working on a plan, though," Milly said.

"I had a feeling you did, big bro. You've always been able to fix problems."

"I am working on a plan, Core, but it's not complete yet. I still have to get a few things figured out before I feel confident enough to escape."

"He's fixing things here already. A toilet and a fan so far. I'm Milly, by the way."

"I'm Corey, Jonah's brother."

"Oh, I know who you are," Milly said.

"Corey, I should probably go ahead and tell you something now. It's going to be hard to believe, but it's true."

"Lay it on me," Corey said.

"Milly is telepathic."

Corey's brow furrowed as he thought it over. "I hate to ask, but can you—"

"Prove it? Sure." Milly closed her eyes and reopened them a couple seconds later. "Think of a number and any color you want."

Corey rubbed his chin, then said, "Okay, got it."

"Think of that number and color in your head. Focus on each of them. It makes it easier for me to hear it." Milly closed her eyes again. "Seventy-four and orange."

Corey's jaw dropped. "No way. That's incredible. Do those people know she can read minds?"

"No, they don't. And we can't let them know," I said. "Just like we can't let them know that I know you guys. They could use you against me somehow."

"Yeah, but they know me and Zane know each other."

"I know. Did you see how they used you against Zane to get your name?"

"Yeah. This is all just so crazy." Corey looked around the room. "Damn, they even have cameras on us."

"They can't hear us, though," Milly said.

"She's right. I've been in the room they use for surveillance. They have me fixing a ceiling fan in there."

"You should eat your food, Corey," Milly said.

Corey got to his feet and grabbed the bread and water from the plastic tray. As he stood at the front of his cell, examining the food, he said, "Water and bread. Looks like something Dad would make us for dinner."

"Speaking of Dad, how is he?"

"Oh. He's worried about you, all right."

"Really?"

"Yeah, he called the police station, and they told him there was no record of you being arrested."

"Then what?"

"He reported you missing. Zane told me you were turning yourself in, but when we found out you didn't make it to the police station, me and Zane went out looking for you. That's how we ended up here. There was a girl on the side of the road. She was—"

"Lying on the shoulder of the road, not moving, right?" I said.

"Yeah. How'd you know?"

"That's how they got me. Bruce and Enzo pushed my bike over, and that girl on the side of the road wasn't just some damsel in distress. It was Dr. Truex."

"The goth chick?" Corey asked.

"That's the one," I said. "Here, catch." I stuck my arm out of my cell and threw the apple back to Corey. Being the baseball star that he was, he caught it effortlessly.

"Thanks," he said.

"You look like you could use it," I said, watching as he went to the sink to wash the apple. "Oh, and don't antagonize these people. Just play along. Act like you really believe the crap they're telling us. Trust me, it's a lot easier that way."

"They already don't like you much, Corey. I heard their thoughts, and none of what they were thinking was good," Milly said. "When they take you back to get your blood, do as they say."

"Okay, but—"

The door opened, and Bruce came in the room first. He was holding a plastic cup and seemed annoyed about something, but then again, Bruce always looked that way. He yelled down the hall for Enzo. "Hurry up, will ya?"

"I'm walkin' as fast as I can. Not my fault the kid passed out," Enzo said as he walked into the room with Zane thrown over his shoulder like a sack of flour.

We all watched silently as Enzo laid Zane on his cot. Bruce handed Enzo the plastic cup. He set it down next to Zane's limp body.

Bruce made eye contact with Milly and said, "When he wakes up, tell him to sip on that soda."

Milly shook her head to show she understood, then looked at me. She looked terrified. I figured she must have read Bruce's mind. I'd probably be terrified if I knew what was going on in his head, too.

"Okay, string bean, I got the new ceiling fan. You're coming with me, and the new guy is going with Enzo to get his blood taken," Bruce said, then glanced over at Corey. "You're not going to give us any trouble now, are you?"

"No. No, sir, I'm not," Corey said.

"Good. Because if you do, I'll have to take extreme measures this time."

"Won't be necessary."

Bruce unlocked Corey's cell first, then mine. Enzo went into the cell and cuffed Corey, and Bruce came into mine and grabbed me by the back of my shirt, saying, "I don't need to cuff you, do I, string bean?"

"No, sir. Not unless you feel the need to do so."

"I think we'll be just fine." Bruce nodded his head at Enzo. "Okay, let's go. And remember, newbie, don't try any funny business."

"I won't," Corey said, meeting my eyes for a second before being led away from me.

For a brief moment, I watched Enzo lead my brother toward the White Room. I feared the worst and felt my stomach churn under the tight shirt I was wearing. Bruce still had it gripped tight from the back. We walked out of the room that housed our cells, then he opened the door to the surveillance room, pushing me inside and releasing his hold on me.

"Okay, string bean, the screwdriver is on the chair underneath the ceiling fan. The new fan is in that box over there. Work your magic," Bruce said as he held one hand on the doorknob.

"Bruce, before you go, I need you to do something."

He squinted at me and said, "Yeah? Well, I need you to do something, too. Fix that ceiling fan before I lose my patience."

"Sir, I just need the breaker to this room turned off. I could get electrocuted otherwise."

Bruce scoffed at my request, then added, "Anything else you need, prince pain-in-the-ass?"

I almost grinned but stopped myself. "A flashlight would be helpful, if you happen to have one handy."

Annoyed, Bruce slammed the door shut. I heard him lock the door and walk away from the room. I listened until I could no longer hear his footsteps slapping against the concrete floor. I wasn't sure if he'd actually turn the breaker off for me or not. I was doubtful that he'd supply me with a flashlight, but I decided to wait a few minutes to see if he would.

In the meantime, I went to the door on the other side of the room—the one that led to the place resembling a living room. I went to turn the knob, only this time it was locked. I examined the doorknob and striker plate and found that it was one I wouldn't be able to unlock with my screwdriver or any tool other than the key that fit the lock.

After this discovery, I went back to the other part of the room, where the monitors were set up. On the screen, I saw Milly lying on her cot. She was reading her book and was most likely imagining she was anywhere but here.

I went over to the box that the new ceiling fan was in and opened it up. It had a bronze housing with cherrywood blades that had to be fastened once the housing was hung and wired. It was basic, but not a bad choice. As I began to pull it out of the box, the light in the room went out. Bruce had turned the breaker off for me. I immediately realized I would need that flashlight I had mentioned before, because now the room was pitch black. I reached around until I felt the chair and sat there until Bruce came in the room. A few minutes went by, and the door opened. As light spilled into the room from the hallway, I saw that Bruce was holding a flashlight in his left hand.

"Okay, string bean, if you need anything else, you're out of luck."

"Guess I can't get you to hold the flashlight for me?"

"So damn needy. I'm going to go switch jobs with Enzo. He can hold the stupid flashlight. Stay put."

Bruce left the room. I heard him walk down the hallway to the White Room. I could hear Bruce's muffled voice say something, then a door close, followed by someone walking back toward the room I was in. As the door began to open, I heard, "Hey, vato."

"What's up, Enzo?"

"So, Bruce wants me to hold a flashlight for you or somethin'?"

"Yeah, I can't undo the wiring and then wire up the new ceiling fan while holding a flashlight. I'll need someone to hold the light for me."

"I got you."

Enzo shined the light on the ceiling fan, and I began disassembling it and taking the old one down. I hung the new one up and began to wire it, finishing each wire with a wire nut. Before too long, I had the new ceiling fan up and wired. I just needed to make sure everything was connected correctly before installing the new fan blades.

"Hey, Enzo, do you know where the panel box is?" I asked.

"Yeah, of course. What you need?"

"I'd like to make sure everything is wired right and working before installing these fan blades. If it works, I won't need you to hold that flashlight anymore."

"Okay, I'll be right back." Enzo closed the door and walked down the hallway. Dull-minded Enzo hadn't thought to lock the door or cuff me to anything like Bruce had done last night. Bruce hadn't given his eye-patched colleague the keys to lock the door, but Enzo did have cuffs on him, and he chose not to use them on me. I wasn't a fan of Enzo, but I'd admit that I favored him over Bruce.

I remembered it taking Bruce a few minutes to flip the breaker to this room. I knew it would take Enzo that long—if not longer—to find the panel box and flip the breaker back on. I grabbed the knob and slowly opened the door, looking out both ways. To my right was the room that housed Milly, Corey, Zane, and me. To the left was the White Room. I wanted so badly to just leave this place, to find a way out. I couldn't leave everyone behind, though. Sure, I could come back with the police, but as soon as they realized I was gone, they'd kill everyone and relocate.

Something told me to go to the White Room, though. I walked down the hallway on the tips of my toes. Behind the door would be my brother, presumably having his blood taken. I was only a few feet from the door when I heard Corey screaming in the White Room.

Chapter 19

My first instinct was to kick the door in and help my brother. I thrust my leg out but stopped the bottom of my foot only inches from the door. If I kicked the door in, then what? Was I going to single-handedly take down Bruce and an insane doctor with all sorts of sharp objects to stab me with? As hard as it was for me to do, I waited and listened.

"Take it easy. I'm just getting a few vials of your blood for samples." It was Dr. Truex's voice. "I took you for the tough one of the bunch, but you're screaming like a child over a little needle."

I heard Corey say, "I don't like needles. Never have. They always hurt like hell."

I remembered Corey screaming like that every time he ever got a shot. It was true: he hated needles.

I was glad I hadn't kicked the door in over that. I also realized that Enzo would be back soon, and if I wasn't in that room, whether Enzo liked me or not, I'd be dead. I rushed back to the room on my tiptoes and closed the door softly behind me. The light in the room was on, which meant the breaker had been flipped back on and that I had wired the fan up properly. At once, I began to install the fan blades on the ceiling fan.

A minute or so later, Enzo opened the door and walked in. "Hey, you got it workin'. Nice. That fan has been busted for a long time, man."

"Yeah, nothing to it," I said, continuing to install the fan blades.

"How much longer till you're done, vato?"

"Five minutes, give or take."

"Okay, good. Bruce said he had somethin' else he wanted you to look at."

"Any idea what that could be?"

"No, he didn't say."

"Enzo, can I ask you something?" I asked, not meeting his eyes as I worked on the fan.

"Yeah, sure."

"I know Bruce has been here longer, but do you think he'll always bully you around and tell you what to do?" I knew I was bringing up a touchy subject, but if my plan was going to work, I would need Enzo to procure Bruce's keys one way or another.

"He don't bully me, vato. I do what he asks of me because he's..." Enzo paused, seeming uncertain. "He's like the manager here."

"But he's not your boss, right?" I asked, stopping what I was doing to look at him.

"No, he's not. The doctor signs my checks... Well, gives me cash on Fridays."

"Ah, I see. So, he manages you, then?"

"I don't really look at it like that. I don't really like how that sounds, either."

"I just think he should trust you with the keys and with other stuff, too. You know, like other than just bringing in our food. I mean, you're not a lunch lady. Far from it. You think that's how he thinks of you, Enzo?"

Enzo put his head down and rubbed his chin with his thumb and index finger. When he looked back up, he said, "You know, sometimes it does feel like he thinks I'm his little errand boy. He had me go get that ceiling fan for you, vato. Then he took the credit for getting it. Pisses me off that he always wants to take the credit but wants none of the blame when he messes up."

"What's he not taking the blame for?"

"He's just— It doesn't matter. Just fix that stupid fan so I can get you back into your cell."

"Sure thing," I said, then started to work on the fan again. "You know, my old boss could be like that sometimes, too."

"Just shut up. I don't want to—"

The door behind Enzo opened, and Bruce came in, twirling the keys on his index finger like a jailer. "You about done with that fan? I got something else for you, string bean," Bruce said, then looked at Enzo. "Dr. Truex wants you to go clean the counters and sweep the floor in her examination room."

I glanced at Enzo. I could tell that his teeth were clenched tight behind his closed mouth. I expected steam to come pluming out of his ears like a character in an old cartoon, but of course that didn't happen. He stared down at the floor and walked briskly past Bruce without saying a word.

Bruce wore a disconcerting grin on his face. He narrowed his eyes and said, "You ready to fix some more stuff, string bean?"

"Yeah, it's the least I could do since you guys are trying to cure the disease I have." It was difficult for me to say that last bit with a straight face.

"You're darn right about that," he said, smacking my upper back. "Come on. Follow me this way."

He ambled toward the White Room, and I wondered just what in the hell he needed me to do in there. I began to panic, knowing that Ronnie had died in that room. I thought this might be a ploy to operate on me, so I hesitated.

"Hey, get the lead out of your ass and get over here," Bruce said by the White Room's door. His smile was gone, and his tone had changed to a deeper, meaner one.

"Sorry," I said, because that was all I could think to say.

I forced myself to walk to him. It wasn't like I had much of a choice. He led me through the door, and at once I smelled the strong odor of bleach. To my left, I saw that Enzo was in the room, already cleaning and sanitizing the countertops. He didn't even look at us as we walked past him.

"Okay," Bruce said, pointing to the door in the corner of the room. "I need to see if you can fix the light in this room. It went out on us this morning."

"Bad bulb?" I asked, then watched as Bruce's face twisted into a scowl.

"You think I didn't already try that? Think I'm stupid or something?"

"No, sorry. I'll check it out."

He scoffed and had me follow him to the door. He dug the keys out of his front pocket and unlocked it. The room was dark, and I wasn't able to see in it very well. All I could make out in the scant light were several shelves lined against the room's walls, along with a large white box in the middle of everything.

Bruce tried flipping the light switch on a dozen times, looking around at the ceiling as if the light were hiding somewhere. "See, damn light won't work. And yes, it has a new bulb," he said, meeting my eyes. "So it ain't that."

"Hmm, can I give it a try?" I asked.

"Knock yourself out."

I grabbed the switch and flipped it on and off a couple times. When nothing happened, I turned the switch on and wiggled it left and right. It flickered a few times, and when I held it in a certain spot, it stayed on. When I observed what was in the room, I could not believe what I was looking at. Various organs were preserved in jars on shelves throughout the entire room. I saw livers, kidneys, a few human hearts, and even a couple of brains. The large white box in the middle of the room was, in fact, a deep freezer. I assumed that it didn't contain steak or any other kind of animal meat inside of it. I actually thought I might puke because of the nightmare I was seeing before me, but I managed not to somehow.

When I spun around to look at Bruce, he appeared to be flabbergasted by how I had made the lights work. It was as if I had just performed some unbelievably clever magic trick before his very eyes. And even though I was in a room teeming with human organs, I couldn't help but be amused by the dumb look on Bruce's face.

"I'll be damned. How'd you know to do that?" Bruce asked me, still in awe.

"Something I learned from my boss."

"That was incredible. I can't believe you figured it out so fast."

"Yeah, just needs a new light switch. You pick one up, and I'll be able to install it in a matter of minutes. I'll just need a couple screwdrivers and the breaker flipped again."

"We can do that, string bean. Yes, we can. There anything you can't fix, kid?"

"Well, I don't have a cure for this disease I have. I don't know how to fix that."

Bruce looked at me for a few moments. I wasn't sure if he felt sorry for me or if maybe he thought I was being sarcastic. Soon, his lip curled up, and he said what was on his mind. "Don't you worry about that. Dr. Truex is the best in the biz. I know this place seems bad, being stuck in a cage and all. We just don't have the funds to keep each patient quarantined in fancy, state-of-the-art rooms, eating steak and lobster. It's just not in the budget."

"I understand, sir. You won't hear any complaining from me."

"You know, string bean, when you first got here, I thought you'd be troublesome like that new guy we got," he said, chuckling. "But you know what? You're all right."

"Well, when I first got here, I didn't understand that you guys were trying to help me. I didn't know about the disease I had. And don't worry about that new guy. I'll talk to him and help him understand why we're here."

"That'd be swell. You do that and tell him to stop resisting. I don't want to have to hurt the little twerp," Bruce said, grinning down at me. He grabbed me by the shoulder and led me out of the room. "Come on. I think it's about time we get you back to your cell."

As I was being led through the White Room, I surveyed the place without Bruce noticing. An idea hit me like a Major League fastball to the head. The White Room contained plenty of sharp objects. I wasn't sure if the room had cameras, but if it did, they'd be inoperable with the breaker flipped. If I could procure something to injure—or perhaps even kill—Bruce or Enzo with, I could execute my plan. A scalpel would suffice, so long as Dr. Truex had enough and wouldn't notice one missing, but I would have to be careful.

I was one step closer to getting this plan of mine figured out.

I heard voices abruptly stop when Bruce opened the door to the room our cells were in. Milly, Corey, and Zane watched as Bruce led me to my cell and locked it once I stepped inside. Bruce didn't say anything to anyone, but he did shoot a look of contempt in Corey's direction. Corey cast his eyes down to avoid the bearded brute's hateful stare.

As soon as Bruce closed the door behind him, Milly spoke up. "Jonah, while you were gone, I filled Zane in on everything."

"That's great," I said. "What about the telepathy thing?"

Zane grabbed the cell bars and pressed his face softly against them. Doing this helped him get a better view of my cell. "Yeah, she even proved it. Corey also told me it was true when he got back from... What did you call it again, Milly?"

"The White Room."

"Yeah, that's where they killed Ronnie," I said.

"Who's Ronnie?" Corey and Zane asked simultaneously.

"Ronnie used to be in that cell to the left of Milly," I said, choosing not to mention the boy named Louis, who had died in Zane's cell.

"He was such a nice man," Milly said, glancing at the empty cell next to her.

It was quiet for a minute or two. Zane was looking around the room and in his cell. My guess was that he was trying to find some magical way out of here. He looked tired and scared as he sat on his bunk. I imagined we all shared that same look.

A few minutes went by, and Corey asked me if I had any updates on my plan to get us out of here. I thought about the light switch I had to install, about whether or not I could find a sharp tool to wound or perhaps even kill our assailants with. Then I bit my lip, suddenly remembering all the human organs I'd seen displayed in that room. I wondered to myself if I should tell them what I had discovered. I knew they were scared, and I didn't want to scare anyone even more. And then—

"Jonah, are you okay? Can you hear me?" I heard Corey ask.

I glanced up to meet his eyes. "Sorry, Core. I was just thinking of something."

"Thinking of what?"

I was reluctant to respond, and that made Corey push harder. "If it's something we need to know, you ought to tell us," he said.

"He's right, Jonah. We need to know what's going on," Milly said.

I watched Zane to see if he was going to urge me to tell what I knew, but he continued to look around the room for a way out.

"You guys really want to know what I have on my mind?"

Milly shook her head, and Corey said, "Yes, spill it, big bro."

"You'll probably want to stay seated for this," I said, then told them about the room full of human organs in jars.

I told them about how I'd look for something sharp that could help us defend ourselves. I told them that I wasn't sure how I'd sneak it back in this room without them noticing, and I told them that I didn't know when Bruce would even get the new light switch.

"Maybe you could sneak whatever you get in your sock," Zane said.

I hadn't thought he'd been paying attention, but obviously he was. "Yeah, that would probably work. They normally don't pat me down or check to see if I have anything on me."

"Shhh," Milly said, her eyes distant. "Someone's coming down the hallway."

When we got quiet, I heard the footsteps, too. I checked the clock on the wall and noticed that it was noon. Enzo should be in at any moment with our lunch.

Seconds later, Enzo came in the room holding trays with our food spread out on them. He worked his way around the room, setting the trays down in front of each cell. He got to me last and said, "Yo, Jonah, guess who has to go pick up that light switch tonight?"

"You?" I asked.

"It figures, man. Bruce's lazy ass said he has other work-related plans tonight. You think he's lyin'?"

"I think you know he is, Enzo."

I could tell he was gritting his teeth. After a moment or two of thought, Enzo said, "I'm sick of this. Dude needs to get his own light switch tonight. I had plans of my own. You know what I'm sayin'?"

"Tell him you already have plans."

"Oh, I'm going to, vato. Damn right I am. I'll check you later," Enzo said, then exited the room without saying another word.

I bent down and picked the tray up. It was the same old apple, bread, and water combination. At least the bread hadn't been saturated in toilet water this time. I took a bite out of the apple and saw Corey watching me.

"Jonah, are you friends with that guy?" he asked.

I lowered my voice in case Enzo was near the room. I didn't want him to know about my plan to gain his trust or about how I really despised him deep down. "It's just a ruse, Core. A ruse that will encourage Enzo to be as careless as possible. I need him that way for my plan to work. I also need him to get the keys to the place from Bruce, one way or another. Bruce probably wouldn't fall for what I'm thinking about doing, so Enzo is our best shot."

"Ah, I see. So you *have* gotten further along in your plan."

"I have. But it's not foolproof. Far from it."

"What do you have so far?" Milly asked, looking hopeful.

"Well, as you've just heard, I'll need Enzo to get the keys. Then I'll have to incapacitate him somehow. If I can't do that, I'll have to...kill him."

"You...you think you'll be able to...you know...when the time comes?" Zane asked.

"In here, Zane, I don't have any other choice. It's us or them."

He nodded and sat on his cot, running his hands through his hair.

"I'll do it for you if you want me to," Corey said.

"No," I said, meeting his eyes. The swelling around his eye, where Bruce had struck him, had gone down some already.

"Are you sure? I can—"

"It has to be me, Core. I'm the only one he halfway trusts."

Corey nodded his head. "Okay, big bro. If you say so."

After the conversation, everyone did their own thing for a while. Milly went back to reading her book, Corey was doing pushups every so often, and Zane stared at the ceiling as he rested on his cot. I tried to read the book I had, but my thoughts wouldn't allow me to focus. I wanted to escape from this place, but this time I didn't want to escape into a good book. I needed a real escape this time, because time was ticking, and sooner or later they were going to cut one of us open and take out an organ or two. I couldn't let that happen to anyone here.

When they supplied me with the new light switch to install in that room, I'd have to come back with something. I wasn't exactly sure what that something would be, but I did have an idea. Whether it was a good idea or not, I didn't know. But as I sat there on my cot, thinking it over in my head, I realized there was only one thing I could really do other than execute my plan to the best of my ability.

Hope.

Chapter 20

According to the analog clock on the wall, it was getting close to dinnertime. Time dragged on and on in these cells. Every minute felt like an hour had just passed. Thankfully, I was given a brief respite from confinement. Every time they needed something fixed, I was able to get out of that dreaded room and go into another. Even though I was put to work, it was still better than being locked in a cage all the time.

I understood why they didn't want to hire someone on the outside to do the jobs. This place wasn't here for other people to know about. I believed that we were hidden deep in the woods—a place that people would never expect to exist. I believed that because, when I looked out of that little window in the steel door, all I could really see were trees and greenery. No paved roads in sight. I had a feeling we were still in Tampa somewhere, though, or at least close to it.

When people thought of Tampa, they thought of buildings and traffic everywhere, and they were not wrong. There was plenty of that. But those people would be surprised by what existed on the outskirts of the city. Mostly, you'd find parks or a preserve if you drove around. However, on certain backroads, you'd discover that all wasn't as it seemed. There *were* heavily wooded areas, and I was almost positive we were in one of them. One that, if people went poking around in it, they ended up in a cell, being told that they had an extremely rare disease.

I pushed myself up from my cot and looked up at the clock on the wall, realizing I had been thinking to myself for nearly an hour. To my left, I heard Milly whisper, "Jonah, I think Corey is upset. He's thinking too much over there. I tried not to listen to his thoughts, but they are just so loud. I couldn't help but hear."

"That's okay, Milly. I'll talk to him. How are you, though?"

She smiled a little and said, "I'm just ready to get out of here and see my parents. I miss them so much." Tears formed in her eyes, but they didn't fall. She wiped them away with the palms of her hands when the room's door opened.

Enzo came in holding a few books, and he made his way over toward Corey and Zane. "Sup, vatos."

Neither Zane nor Corey said a word. Zane looked like a dog that was afraid it might be beaten. Corey just sat on his cot, hunched over, his elbows on his knees, staring at the concrete floor.

"You guys deaf all of a sudden?" Enzo asked.

"No, sir," Corey said, not looking up.

"Good. You guys want a book to read or somethin'? I got playing cards, too."

"I'll take a book if that's okay," Zane said.

"Which one you want?" Enzo asked, showing him the book titles.

"I'll take that one," Zane said, pointing to *Cogan's Trade* by George V. Higgins.

Enzo gave him the book and ambled over to Corey, who was still looking at the concrete floor.

"Well, do you want a book or what? I ain't got all day," Enzo said.

"No, sir," Corey said, not making eye contact.

Enzo watched Corey for maybe ten seconds. When Corey didn't look at him, Enzo said, "You got a problem? If so, I can come in there and black your other eye for you."

Corey's eyes shot up to meet Enzo's, and I feared his retort would only get him hurt worse. I didn't know if I could watch that again without screaming my lungs out.

Corey said, "No, sir. I don't have a problem. I didn't mean any disrespect."

Corey glanced at me for a second before looking at the concrete floor again. It was obvious that he was miserable. I hated to see him that way.

All of us in the room handled this plight in a different way. However, the consensus between the four of us was that we hated where we were and wanted out.

Enzo glanced at me and then back to my brother. "Jonah set you straight, didn't he?" he asked Corey.

"Yeah, I guess you could say he did. I didn't realize you guys were here to help us at first," Corey said.

He was still looking down, smirking now, though. Enzo wasn't able to see him smirking from where he was standing, but a ping of unease still ran through my stomach. I knew that if Core got caught, Enzo wouldn't hesitate to beat him down again.

"Of course we're here to help. Why else would you be here?" Enzo asked.

I felt that Enzo was setting my brother up. Like he was trying to get Corey to say something smart. From my perspective, Enzo badly wanted to get in there and rough Corey up. I hoped like hell Core wouldn't take the bait.

Before Corey could respond, I said, "That's right. My pal Enzo is many things, but a liar isn't one of them."

Enzo turned around and glared at me. At first glance, he had that crazed look about him, but then his expression changed to one that was almost amiable. "Thanks, Jonah. But I didn't ask for you to vouch for me, did I?" His crazed look came back as fast as it had disappeared.

"Sorry," I said.

Enzo began to walk toward my cell. He looked pissed, like I had just pelted him with a baseball or something. Then he took a deep breath and whispered, "Look, man, I didn't mean to be like that toward you. I'm just tired of Bruce makin' me do his job. He's supposed to get that switch tonight, not me. One of these days, I feel like I'm gon' snap on him. You feel me?"

"I understand, Enzo. It's all good."

Enzo did something I never thought he would ever do: he stuck his closed fist in my cell for a fist bump. And I, of course, gave him one. I had his trust, and it made me feel much better about getting out of here.

"See ya around dinnertime," Enzo said, then headed out of the room without even a quick glance at Corey.

I was relieved to see that my distraction had worked and that my brother hadn't been injured any more.

"Hey, Core," I said.

"Yeah, Jonah?"

"What's going on in that head of yours?"

"Too much to tell."

"Well, we have time. It's not like we're getting out of here tonight."

He looked at the concrete floor and stopped talking.

"Come on, Core. Don't make Milly tell us what's really on your mind."

When Corey lifted his head up to look at me, I noticed that his eyes were shiny with unshed tears. "I just feel so bad for Dad. He's lost Mom, he's worried sick about you, and now he's probably worried about me and Zane. A man can only take so much, you know?" He was doing his best to speak without losing his composure. "Jonah, what if we don't get out? What if we die here?"

It took me a minute to respond. I'd had that same exact thought run through my head at least a dozen times since I'd been here. I wondered if my dad would be okay. I wondered if he would just give up on life and fall apart mentally—or worse, end his own life. I'd thought about so many things in this cell, and I still hadn't come up with an adequate answer to most of them. Especially this one.

I said the only thing I could think to say. It was the truth. "I don't know, Core. I do know one thing, though."

Corey wiped the tears away and waited for what I would say next.

"I know Mom and Dad would want us to fight. They'd want us to fight like hell. And that's what I plan on doing. Whether we get out of here or not, we're going to at least make them wish they had picked other people to capture and stick in cages."

I looked around the room, and everyone was smiling a little, even my brother.

"I miss my parents, too," Milly said, looking at Corey. "I'd do anything to see them again."

"My parents are probably losing their minds, too," Zane said. "If only we had a way to call the police from in here."

"Even if we were able to, I don't know if that'd be the best thing to do. I feel like if they knew the police were coming here, they'd kill us, pack up any evidence, and flee to their next secluded location to start up the same old scheme," I said.

"I didn't think of that," Zane said. "Dude, this sucks worse than a worn-out vacuum."

We all chuckled in spite of our situation. We were four immensely unfortunate people, but then again, we were still alive. I told myself that as soon as I got that weapon, whatever it may be, I'd plan our escape for that very night. We didn't have time to waste.

Who knew that something as simple as knowing how to change a light switch would play such a pivotal role in our staying alive?

Chapter 21

It was almost dinnertime, and I was sick of the water, bread, and apple diet. I craved pizza and wings but knew I wouldn't get any. In this place, you didn't get a last meal like you did in prison. Ronnie was proof of that. In here, you got dragged out by two large men, thrown on an operating table, and sentenced to death by an inept doctor who was selling your organs for a high price to other criminals abroad.

I didn't plan on sticking around long enough for that to happen, but the scary thing here was that we had no way of knowing when Dr. Truex would call our numbers. Sooner or later, Bruce or Enzo would come through that door and take one of us, just like they took Ronnie. Maybe we would make it through the first surgery—hell, maybe even the second one, too—but as soon as they got all they could from us, we'd be thrown away like last night's pasta casserole.

When Enzo came into the room, he held trays with the usual on them: water, bread, and apples. Only this time, I noticed something else on the trays: Styrofoam cups with some kind of liquid in them. When he made his rounds, he got to me last, as usual.

"Here you go, vato," Enzo said, setting the tray on the floor in front of my cell. "Eat up. There's some chicken broth for you guys tonight."

"What's the occasion?" I asked.

"Don't worry about that. Just enjoy," he said. "Oh. Bruce told me to tell you to be ready to fix that light switch tomorrow morning after breakfast."

"No problem. I'll be ready."

Enzo grinned and quickly left the room.

He usually isn't in such a hurry, I thought. Then I remembered that he needed to go to the hardware store to get a new light switch for tomorrow morning. I still found it a bit strange, but maybe he had plans tonight. It was weird to think of Enzo having a life outside of being one of Dr. Truex's goons, but it was apparent that he had something on his mind.

As I sipped on the warm chicken broth, I began to wonder what he did when he wasn't here. My guess was that he worked out and worked on that car he was always talking about. I thought it was so unfair for someone like him to be out there while we were struck in here waiting to die. I wondered what I had done to deserve this, then soon pondered why any of us deserved this. I got emotional, just as Corey had, but I didn't let the others see me upset. I ate the food Enzo gave me, and then I sat on my cot, reading my book until it was time to go to sleep.

That night, I dreamed of a day that had scarred Corey and I for life. The dream was based off a time when we actually went to Daytona Beach, back when my brother and I were just kids. We knew we were good swimmers at the time, but as it turned out, we were not as good as we had thought. Each of us ran into the water, side by side, laughing and having the time of our lives until the rip current took us under. It was the first time in my short life that I had realized I wasn't indestructible, that I easily could have died that day.

I heard the rushing of water tossing and turning me in different directions, along with muffled shouts coming from above. I felt my heart hammering in my chest as my lungs starved for oxygen. Before I drowned in the saltwater of Florida's Atlantic coast, though, my mother pulled me out of the rip current by my upper arm, and I was able to breathe again. I was crying, and so was she. To my left, I saw that my dad had Corey in his arms, holding him as he cried, as well.

Then my dad's appearance began to change, almost like he was melting into something else. I blinked and suddenly saw Bruce and Enzo holding my brother above the water one second, then shoving him under the next, laughing. I looked at my mom so I could tell her to help Corey, but when I saw the woman holding me, it wasn't my mom. It was Dr. Truex. She said, "Don't you worry, little Jonah. They're just fixing him. He'll be good as new in no time."

"No!" I shouted at the top of my lungs. "You're killing him. Stop! Please stop!"

Dr. Truex kissed my forehead, looked at me as if she loved me, and then forced me under the water. I wasn't able to breathe again, and I panicked.

From underneath me, I heard my name being called by a familiar voice. It was a young girl's voice.

"Milly?"

"Jonah, wake up. It's just a dream. Wake up."

My eyes opened, but all I could see was darkness and the four red blinking lights that were always there.

"Milly?" I said again, unsure if she was the one trying to wake me up or not.

"You were moving a lot and making noises. It sounded like you couldn't breathe," Milly said. "Are you okay?"

"Yeah, I'm fine. Just had a bad dream."

"About almost drowning at the beach, right?"

"That's right. My mother pulled me out of the rip current, and she changed—"

"Into Dr. Truex."

"Yeah."

"Sorry, I didn't want to. But when I heard you moving around and making those noises, I had to see what was going on in your head...just to make sure it was a dream and that you weren't having a seizure or something."

"I understand, Milly. Thank you for waking me up. It was a horrible dream."

"You're welcome. It was a difficult dream for me to see, too. I didn't want it to go on and get worse."

"Have you had any bad dreams since you've been here?"

"I don't know. I haven't been able to remember any of them."

"Oh," I said. Then we sat in silence for maybe a minute or two. "Milly, can you see what Corey is dreaming about? I'm just curious...and a little worried about him."

She didn't respond and was silent for a short while. I thought she might have fallen back asleep, but then I heard, "He's dreaming about baseball." Then, a few seconds later, "He has on a shirt that says 'Rays' across the front. The rest is just him playing the game. He hits the ball over the fence and in the stands. The fans are cheering him on...and I see your parents. They're in the stands cheering for him. They're clapping and shouting his name, and you're right there next to them. You're cheering, too."

Now I was the one who was silent. I just kept thinking to myself that I needed to get us out of here somehow. I didn't want to die, but I would if it meant that Corey, Zane, and Milly could get out of here alive and well. Corey had a bright future ahead of him, and that wouldn't happen if he died here. Zane was here because of me, and for that reason I felt obligated to get him out of here alive. And Milly was just too young to be in a place like this. I knew she missed her parents more than anything, and I'd be damned if I didn't get her to them one way or another. Tomorrow was the day, I told myself. I'd wait until dinnertime, when Enzo brought our food, and then I would do what I had to do with whatever I procured from Dr. Truex's White Room. It wasn't the best plan, but under the circumstances it would have to do.

"We're getting out of here tomorrow," I whispered.

"Really? But how, Jonah?"

"I'll tell everyone tomorrow around lunchtime. I still need to do some thinking, but we're getting out of here."

"I'm scared, Jonah. What if the plan doesn't work?"

I knew she knew the answer to that question as well as I did, and if she read my mind, she'd know that I had no idea. It could go well, or it could go bad. I felt that with all the bad luck the four of us had had recently, maybe we were due for some good in the near future.

"Only time will tell," I said. "Get some rest, okay?"

"Jonah, it's not easy always knowing what people are thinking."

I sensed that she knew what I had been thinking. Nothing got past her when she focused. I wasn't happy that she was here, but I was glad that she was on our team.

"I suppose it wouldn't be."

She didn't respond, and this time, based on the sound of her steady breaths, I was sure she had drifted off to sleep. Focusing on Corey's thoughts must've mentally drained her. I took a deep breath, inhaling the room's musty scent.

Tomorrow, I thought just before I fell asleep.

Tomorrow.

Chapter 22

I woke up the next morning when the room's bright lights flickered a few times before staying illuminated above me. I heard the old electric humming sound coming from the lights and watched the others as they woke up. Everyone's eyes were half-lidded as they sat up in their cots, except for Milly's. Her eyes were large and round and something else completely. She glanced at me for a second. Then her gaze slid away as Enzo came into the room. He held no food tray this morning, and that was when I understood why she looked the way she did. She knew something.

"All right, your breakfast will be here shortly, but first Dr. Truex wants Jonah to install that new light switch right away," Enzo said. He didn't seem like himself as he stood there with his arms crossed, staring at me impassively.

"Everything okay?" I asked.

"I'm just waiting for Bruce to get here with the keys."

I felt the urge to check on Milly again but decided against it at that moment. The very next second, Bruce came in holding his keys and walked toward me. He opened my cell and shoved the new light switch into my hand. "This should work, shouldn't it, string bean?" I looked down and saw that they had purchased the right one, and I was glad they had. (If not, I might not be here writing this.) "Yes," I said, looking the switch over. "This will do just fine."

"Wonderful," Bruce said. "Now let's get moving."

Bruce didn't cuff me. He had me lead the way this time since I knew how to get there. He took his keys out and unlocked the door while keeping an eye on me. He didn't trust me *that* much. The door pushed open easily, and I walked into the White Room feeling sick to my stomach, as I always did when entering it. I headed to the storage room in the corner. When I reached the door and opened it, I noticed that Bruce didn't have any tools with him.

"Well, what are you waiting for, string bean? Fix it," he said, his hands on his hips. "The doc wants this light working in here today."

"I'm just going to need a few tools, sir, and the breaker to this room turned off. I really don't want to get electrocuted first thing in the morning, if preventable."

"You're always wanting something, string bean. What all do you need?"

"A screwdriver and flashlight should be all."

"That better be all. You're not going to have me running around twice. You got that?" he said, poking me hard in the chest with his forefinger.

I shook my head.

"Good. Give me your arm."

He retrieved a pair of handcuffs from his back pocket and snapped one of the cuffs around my wrist. He put the other cuff around the leg of a stainless-steel table that was fastened to the concrete floor. Only this time, he cinched the cuff so tight around my wrist that I wouldn't be able to slide it off. My heart sank as I watched him walk away to get the tools and flip the breaker. My plan hadn't gone as I expected it to go, but then again, how many plans ever go as they're supposed to?

For a second or two, I felt that it was all over, but then I looked down and saw only one bolt holding the table down. The other bolt was missing and probably had been for a long time. I bent down and tried to turn the bolt as hard as I could with my free hand. Relief flowed through me like a cold chill when I discovered the bolt was loose. I was able to move it, but it was a slow process. My fingers were tender by the time I had it halfway out, but I kept turning it despite the pain. The lights in the White Room shut off around the time I had the bolt three quarters of the way out. I knew Bruce would be back soon, so I used that fear to continue turning the bolt. My thumb, forefinger, and middle were throbbing like mad, but after another twenty seconds or so, I finally had the bolt out. Then I heard heavy footfalls from the hallway. I saw a beam of light enter the room and hit the far wall of the White Room. Before Bruce was able to shine the light on me, I placed the bolt in my sock so he wouldn't notice it.

A second after I hid the bolt and pulled my pant leg down, Bruce was shining the flashlight in my eyes and chuckling to himself. "There's my little string bean. You better not have been taking a nap in here while I was gone."

"No, sir."

"All right, let's get that cuff off you, kid."

He unlocked the cuff on my wrist and left the other one cuffed to the stainless-steel table's leg. I thought about thinking of another tool I could use to get him out of here for a minute or two, but I also thought he'd pummel me if I asked. I was almost sure he'd cuff me back to the table after the job was finished, anyway.

I knew the window to procure a weapon had just shortened. I felt panicked but didn't show it. At least, not while Bruce was watching me. He gave me the screwdriver and shined the light on the switch. Without hesitating, I removed the cover, took the wires off the old switch, and wired them to the new one. I reinstalled the cover and was finished in no time at all.

"Wow, string bean, that was pretty damn fast, if I do say so myself."

"Nothing to it."

"Well, come back over here so I can cuff you again, and I'll go flip the breaker back on. See if that switch fixed our problem."

I let him cuff me again and waited for him to leave the White Room. As soon as he went around the corner, where I could no longer see him, I lifted the leg of the table and slid the cuff down, wiggling it over the small bracket. I shuffled over toward the open door and didn't hear anyone coming from either direction, so I went over to Dr. Truex's counter and began going through the drawers as quickly as possible. It was difficult to see in the dark, but I managed the best that I could.

I found a lot of random paperwork in the first few drawers. It wasn't until the third drawer that I found a scalpel. The only problem was that there happened to be only one, and I knew she would find it missing sooner rather than later. I continued looking and found suture kits, surgical gloves and masks, nebulizers, and perhaps a hundred empty syringes.

I stopped looking when I found the vials of Midazolam. I remembered hearing her shout that name back when I first met her, which led me to believe that this had to be the drug that had incapacitated me on the side of the road. There were dozens of them, and I didn't think she'd detect that I had taken any for a while. I hurried back to the other drawer and grabbed three syringes to fill with the Midazolam. Since I had no clue what the proper dosage was, I opted to fill them most of the way up. As I began filling the first one, the lights came back on. My hands had not been shaking too bad before, but now they shook as if I had just been drenched in frigid water from head to toe. I filled the other two syringes as fast as I possibly could, then carefully stuffed them all in my other sock, the needles pointed down near the inside of my ankle. The last thing I needed was to inadvertently inject myself with a drug that could incapacitate me.

I knew Bruce would be back in less than a minute, but when I saw Milly's name written across a sheet of paper on the countertop, I had to stop to read it. As I continued to read, I began to feel like hurling up last night's dinner. Dr. Truex would be operating on her soon, and her kidneys—both of them—would be on a plane headed overseas. I stood there looking at that piece of paper for almost too long. When I heard heavy footfalls coming my way, I walked as fast and as quietly as I could over to the stainless-steel table in the corner of the room. I tried to wiggle the cuff back over the bracket, but it was giving me trouble. Bruce was getting closer, his footfalls louder. My heart pumped faster and faster. I was sure I would be caught, but when he came around the corner, my cuff was over the bracket and around the leg of the table, just the way he had left me.

I looked over at the storage room and noticed that the light was working. Bruce had a smile on his face when he saw that the light was on and went over to the room before uncuffing me. He walked in, looked around, and tested the light switch a few times, turning it on and off. When he faced me, his smile was still there, although now it seemed to me that he was smiling for a different reason.

A couple seconds later, I heard more footfalls coming from the hallway, accompanied by the voices of Dr. Truex, Enzo, and Milly.

"Well, it's time to get you back in your cell, string bean. We got some business to take care of right now," Bruce said, taking the cuff off my wrist. "Come on. Let's go."

Bruce pushed me ahead, and I saw Milly being dragged along by Enzo. She was kicking, screaming, and trying to throw herself on the floor. She knew what they were about to do to her. When she saw me in the White Room next to Bruce, she screamed, "Jonah, they're going to kill me. I know they are! I can't—"

Dr. Truex slapped Milly across the face so hard that her nose began to ooze a slow trickle of blood. It was beyond difficult not to intervene. I felt myself tense up, but I remained cool on the outside. On the inside, that wasn't the case.

That slap seemed to have taken some of the fight out of Milly. I thought it had disoriented her to some degree, as well. She stopped resisting as much and allowed Enzo to drag her into the White Room. I had to keep reminding myself to breathe as I watched it all play out in front of me.

Behind me, I was surprised to hear Bruce say, "Enzo, here. Give me the girl. You take Jonah back to his cell. He listens better than this one."

Then I saw my chance. Bruce handed Enzo the keys.

Enzo gladly took them from Bruce. It was obvious that he was taken aback by Bruce finally trusting him enough. Enzo looked at me with a stupid grin on his face, grabbed me by the arm, and said, "Come on, vato. Let's get you back home."

"Yes, let's," I said. Then Enzo led me out of the White Room. I wanted to look back at Milly, but I knew there were too many eyes watching. I wanted to tell her I'd be back for her soon. Then I remembered about her ability, so I thought it in my head and hoped she heard me.

Up ahead, I noticed that the door leading to our holding cells was ajar, which wasn't conducive to my plan at all. I'd have to make it work, though. One way or another, I'd have to make it happen.

I felt the syringes rubbing against the skin on my ankle and tried to think about how I was going to do this. Enzo was much larger and much stronger. I wasn't given a lot of time to work it over in my head, though. Before I knew it, I was standing in front of my cell and Enzo was holding the door open.

"All right, Jonah. In you go," he said, still in a chipper mood.

I walked in and pretended to see something in my cell. "Did you see that? Something just moved behind the toilet, man," I said.

While Enzo looked at the toilet, confused, I nodded at Corey and Zane in a help-me-out-here kind of way.

"I see it, too, Jonah. It just moved," Corey said.

"Dude, be careful," Zane added.

"What the hell are you guys talkin' about?" Enzo asked.

As he walked past me, I reached down and slid the bolt out of my sock, along with a syringe full of Midazolam out of my other one. My hands started to shake again, this time even worse.

Enzo turned out around quickly, grabbed me by the throat, and asked, "What kind of game are you guys playin' here? There ain't nothin' behind that toilet." He shoved me against my cell, and I tossed the bolt at the toilet.

When the bolt struck the porcelain, I heard Corey say, "There it is again!"

Enzo glanced back at the toilet again. He still had me by my throat, and I was struggling to breathe. I doubted I'd get a much better chance than this one, so while he was looking away, I jabbed the syringe into his neck and injected him with as much Midazolam as I could. He screamed and jerked away from me, pulling the syringe out. When he looked at me afterward, I saw one watery eye, flared nostrils, and teeth clenched down so tight that I thought he might crack them if he didn't stop. Before he could grab me, I ran out of the cell and tried to lock him in, but he reached the door before I could. With the adrenaline coursing through me, I was able to give him somewhat of a fight, but he overpowered me and got out of the cell.

"You're dead, vato. You ain't gonna make the table," he said, then rushed toward me.

My back was against the wall, but I noticed something about Enzo when he made that last threatening statement: his speech was slurred, and quite badly. I stood there, like an animal caught in a trap, and waited for him to rush me. I thought that if I was able to duck fast enough, he would crash into the wall, but instead he took a step, then another, and dropped down to his knees. Right before Enzo passed out, he made eye contact with me. He wasn't enraged right before losing consciousness. No, another emotion had stumbled its way into his mind: fear.

I looked down at Enzo. He was a few feet from me. His eye that wasn't concealed by the eyepatch was closed now, and drool had started to run down one side of his mouth. I had no idea if I had given him too much or not, and at that moment I really didn't care. He was out cold, and that was what mattered.

To my right, I heard Corey say something, but I didn't understand him, because my mind was still trying to wrap itself around what had just happened. I looked at Corey and said, "What'd you say?"

He pointed to Enzo's body. "The keys, Jonah. Hurry up and get the keys."

I snapped out of it. "Where are they? Did you see what he did with them?"

"In his front pocket," Zane said. "See if he has a car key on him, too."

"Yeah, then get us the hell out of these cells," Corey added.

I kneeled next to Enzo, rolled him on his back, and searched through his pockets. Underneath the fabric of his jeans, I spotted the lump of keys. I procured them within seconds and then checked the other pocket for the car key. I remembered him saying he had a Subaru. If that was true, I could get us out of here and back to town in no time. In his other pocket, I found not only his car key but also a switchblade knife. When I pressed the button on the handle, a four-inch blade shot out of it.

"Score," Corey said. "Now get us out of here before he wakes up."

"He's right, Jonah. Come on," Zane said, waving me over.

I shoved the Subaru key into my front pocket, along with the knife. There were over a dozen keys on that key ring. I started with the first one, which didn't open the lock to Corey's cell. It wasn't until I reached the seventh key that I got it to unlock the cell. *Lucky number seven*, I thought. After I opened Corey's cell, I hurried over to Zane's and let him out.

"Okay, let's go," Corey said, rushing over to the door.

"Hold on," I said. "We have to get Milly."

"Where is she?" Zane asked.

"In the White Room," I said. "They're going to take her kidneys. I saw the paperwork. I could tell that she knew, too."

"Well, what are we waiting for?" Corey said. "Let's go get her."

I nodded. *I hope they haven't started the surgery yet*, I thought but didn't say.

"What about Bruce?" Zane said. "We can't take that guy."

Corey looked at Zane and grinned. "Of course we can."

I took the knife out of my pocket, pressed the button that released the blade, and said, "We'll have to try."

When the three of us left the room, we started for the door that led to the White Room.

"Wait," I said. "Here, Zane. Take these." I placed the keys into Zane's hand and pointed to the door that led to the surveillance room. "Find the key that unlocks that door. There will be two more doors we have to get through to get out of here."

I could see the sweat on Zane's brow. "You sure about this, Jonah?"

"Trust me," I said. "And be ready for the next two doors. We're going to get Milly and be back as fast as we can."

Zane nodded and began inserting keys to find the correct one. Corey and I rushed over to the White Room's door, but before we went in, I said, "Core, whatever happens, don't worry about me. Get Milly and Zane out of here."

"You know I can't—"

I opened the door and rushed in first.

Chapter 23

The first thing I saw was a large leather strap over Milly's arms and upper body. Her eyes lit up when she saw Corey and I burst in. She tilted her head to the left and said, "She's over there in that room. She'll be back any second. Hurry."

"Core, go close that door and hold it shut so I can free Milly," I said. "I'm on it."

When Corey slammed the door closed, the three of us heard Dr. Truex shout from within. There wasn't a lock on the door, so Corey had to keep it from opening.

I found the buckle on the strap that was restraining Milly and pressed down, loosening the strap enough for her to get up. "Are you okay?" I asked.

"Yeah, but I don't know where Bruce went. He left after he strapped me down."

In the storage room, Dr. Truex stopped shouting and was quiet for a few seconds. Corey looked at us quizzically. Then we heard a cell phone ringing somewhere in the building. It was barely audible, but when we heard it, we knew why she had stopped yelling: she was calling Bruce.

I grabbed Milly by the hand and said, "Core, let's go. We don't have long before Bruce gets here."

He shoved off the door and ran out of the White Room with us. (It was the last time we would ever step foot into that awful room, but I still see it when I close my eyes at night.)

When we entered the hall, we saw Zane up ahead still trying to find the right key.

"Hurry, Zane. They'll be here soon," I said, running toward him.

"I'm moving as fast as I can. None of these keys are opening this stupid—"

The door opened, and they all rushed in before me. I glanced behind me and saw a furious-looking Dr. Truex rushing through the White Room's threshold. To my left, down the other intersecting hallway, I saw Bruce sprinting in my direction, a pistol in his hand. I didn't wait around long enough to see if he'd use it. I entered the room as quickly as I could and locked it behind me.

"Unlock the door up ahead," I said.

"It's already unlocked. Come on. Run!" Zane said.

I locked that door after I went through it, and I heard three gunshots. Everyone stopped to look around. Then I realized why Bruce had fired the gun. He didn't have his keys, and a bullet through the door's lock was the only option he had at the time.

Zane was going through the keys as fast as his shaking hands would allow. He had found the one that unlocked the first deadbolt, and he had already removed the steel rod that didn't require a key. The lock on the second deadbolt was the one we were waiting on.

"Hurry, Zane. They're close. I can hear what they're thinking about, and it doesn't end with us staying alive," Milly said.

We were all at the door behind Zane when gunshots roared from behind us. I heard Bruce trying to twist the knob, and he cussed when it wouldn't open.

"Shoot it again, Bruce! Shoot it again!" Dr. Truex shouted.

I could hear the apprehension in her voice, and it made me smile for a second. It was nice for her to be the one in fear for once.

"Got it!" Zane said as the door swung open.

The sun nearly blinded us as we stormed out of the building. I looked around for the Subaru and didn't see it at first, but then I spotted a blue car behind a black SUV in the distance. From where I was standing, it appeared to be a Subaru. Enzo's Subaru.

I said, "Head for the blue car!"

As I dug my hand into my pocket to retrieve the key, I heard two more gunshots and ran faster than I ever had in my life.

I unlocked the car with the key fob as we ran up to it, and behind us I heard, "Get back here!" It was Bruce, and they had made it out of the building.

I was looking for where to insert the key when Zane pointed to a button on the dashboard and said, "It's a push button, Jonah! Start it! Hurry!"

I pressed the button, and after a one-second delay, the engine started right up. I dropped the transmission into gear and floored it. Rocks spit up from under all four tires. I heard them pelting the inner fender wells as we took off down the only trail I could see.

My heart was pounding harder than when I had been run off the road on my motorcycle. I thought the thrill of getting away was part of it; the other part was when we realized Bruce was still shooting at us. I heard a few bullets hit the car right before the rear window shattered between Corey and Milly. Everyone began to shout, and then I saw Bruce get into the black SUV. From what I could see, maybe fifty yards behind us, Dr. Truex got behind the driver's seat.

I gunned it and went even faster. They were still shouting, but I was too focused on driving and not running us into a tree to realize why they were shouting.

Then Zane's voice made its way in my head, clear and intelligible. "Jonah, Corey's been shot."

Corey had been shot, but I felt like the one who was dying. I lost the ability to breathe until Zane said, "Dude, he was shot in his forearm. He's still alive. Keep driving!"

"I'll be fine, big br—" Corey said, then shouted in pain. "Shit...this hurts!"

"Dammit, Zane, you could have told me that to begin with," I said. "I thought he was dead, man." Then, to Corey, "Core, let me see your arm for a second." He raised it up so I could see it in the rearview mirror. It was bleeding, all right, but it didn't look arterial.

In the back seat, next to Corey, Milly was gripping her knees and looking at me in the rearview.

"Milly, are you okay?" I asked.

She shook her head in quick little movements. "Yeah. Is Corey going to be all right, you think?"

"He will be, but we have to stop his arm from bleeding too much. It looks too dark to have severed an artery, but I think we'd better stanch it just in case."

"How do we do that?" Zane asked.

"A tourniquet," I said, then slid the Subaru around a sharp turn. "Zane, take off your belt and wrap it around his arm, above the wound."

Zane unbuckled his belt as I accelerated, and Corey rested his bleeding arm on the center console. While Zane was putting Corey's arm through the loop he'd made with his belt, I said, "Make sure it's really tight."

Corey winced as Zane cinched the belt around his arm.

"It's as tight as I can get it," Zane said. "I need to make another hole so I can buckle it, though. Jonah, give me the knife in your pocket."

In all the excitement, I had completely forgotten about Enzo's knife. I dug it out of my front pocket as quickly as I could and handed it to Zane. The car was jouncing all over the place as we sped down the long dirt road, but Zane managed to make a hole big enough in the belt for the buckle.

He locked it in and said, "Got it!"

I took another look in the rearview mirror. We were pulling away from Bruce and Dr. Truex. I could no longer see them, and I thought that if we could keep Corey from bleeding out in the backseat of Enzo's car, we would have a chance at living our lives again. Except it wasn't going to be that easy. I noticed that the gas gauge needle was descending at an alarming rate, and I smelled something in the air: gasoline.

I said, "Guys, we're about to run out of gas. I think one of Bruce's bullets hit the gas tank."

Zane had just finished cutting the long piece of excess leather off the makeshift tourniquet. "Are you serious, dude? What the hell are we going to do?"

I looked in the rearview mirror again. Beyond Milly and Corey in the backseat, I still couldn't see Bruce or Dr. Truex in their SUV. "We'll have to ditch the car. Make a run for it. Unless you have a better plan."

Zane shifted in his seat enough to look at Corey and Milly in the backseat of the car. "Please tell me one of you has a better plan."

I heard Corey say, "We could get out and fight them."

"Definitely not," Milly said. "They have a gun, and we don't. And you've been shot."

Zane sighed. "Jonah's plan it is."

I spotted a good place to pull over and hide in the woods up ahead. The tree brush was thick and teeming with foliage on the side of the road we'd be ditching the car, and I thought we wouldn't have a better chance at getting away undetected than this.

"Okay, everyone ready?"

"Now?" Zane asked, bracing himself.

I felt the car starving for fuel and hit the brakes. "Now!"

I threw the car door open and hopped out. Zane and Milly burst out of the car on the passenger side while I made sure Corey was able to run without assistance. He was. He held his wounded arm with his good one while sprinting, and as awkward as he looked, he could still outrun me.

"Where are we going?" Zane asked.

"I don't know," I said as I rushed into the woods. "Just keep running. We need to create some distance between us and them."

I had to duck several times to avoid running face first into low-hanging branches. After a minute or two of running for our lives, my breathing became labored, as did theirs. It didn't take long at all for the Florida humidity to have us sweating from head to toe and gasping for air. I checked behind us and didn't see Bruce or Dr. Truex, but I did hear them. Bruce was shouting and cursing at Enzo for not answering the phone. Dr. Truex was telling him to shut up or else we might hear them. She was right; we did. That was when I decided to stop running straight. That would make it too easy for them to track us.

As I thought about which direction to go in, something occurred to me: if we were to go left from where we were, we'd most likely end up near the place we had escaped. The road we ditched the Subaru on had to have been leading to the hard road. That made the most sense to me, so I went with my gut. (I turned out to be right, but even now I wonder what would have happened if we had ventured left instead.)

Milly was in front of me by perhaps twenty feet. Zane and my brother were a good twenty feet or so from her. I needed to get their attention without being too loud. I continued to run and try to catch up, but they were so much faster. Then, suddenly, I had it. The idea popped into my head, and I didn't waste any time thinking it over.

"Core!" I shouted.

He stopped and spun around, looking at me as if I had lost my mind. "What? We need to keep running."

"Run to the left!" I said, but I repeatedly pointed to the right.

Zane and Milly stopped and turned around when they heard me shout. Their brows were furrowed, and they seemed utterly confused. I didn't blame them. I would have been, too.

"Everyone, to the left! Now!" I continued to point to the right, thrusting my arm that way.

Soon, they understood what I was doing, and I could only hope that Bruce and Dr. Truex would take the bait.

I saw Corey dart off to the right, and the rest of us followed. I had a good feeling that we had thwarted them, that we were finally safe. That feeling didn't stick around very long, but it felt nice while it lasted.

We began to jog and then, once we realized they had fallen for my trick, walk. The adrenaline was still flowing through us, but we had been stuck in cages without any exercise or proper nutrition. I felt my leg muscles cramping up and stopped to stretch them before the muscles could lock up. While performing the stretch, I noticed the syringes in my sock were close to falling out, so I stuffed them back down. I hoped I wouldn't need them, but I wasn't getting rid of them until we were miles away from here.

"You okay, man?" Zane asked me.

With my head still down by my knees in the stretch, I said, "Yeah, just my leg muscles starving for nourishment. Sorry, guys."

"You were in there for longer than us, dude. It's understandable."

"Yeah, I'm pretty sure they fell for your trick, anyway," Corey said.

"They did. I don't hear their thoughts at all now," Milly said. "They have to be going the other direction."

"Good," I said. "I think I'm ready to keep going." I stopped stretching the muscle, and it didn't tighten back up. "Let's go. We need to find a way out of these woods before the sun goes down."

I didn't know how long we walked in those woods that day, but I knew it felt like a lifetime and a half. I supposed it felt like that because we were being hunted by some terrible people. However, I was sure we would reach the road or edge of the woods at some point if we kept on in this direction. And in time we did, but before we could reach it, Corey spotted someone up ahead.

He said, "Guys, it's a police officer! There, just past those trees!"

I squinted and saw the cop in the distance. He was walking toward us now. I was sure he'd heard Corey.

We heard the cop shout, "My name is Officer Cutler. I heard some yelling. Was it you?"

"Yes! We need help! We were kidnapped!" Zane shouted.

"I'm coming. Don't worry. I'll get you to safety!"

I looked at Milly and grinned. "Looks like we're going home."

She smiled and grabbed my hand. "I can't wait to see my parents."

I saw tears in her eyes and a happiness she hadn't had inside of that place. It was a Milly I was seeing for the first time.

As we continued to walk toward the police officer, I saw that he was a shorter man with a flattop haircut. He wore sunglasses, but not the stereotypical aviators you saw cops wearing in movies. These were wayfarers.

"Are you guys— Whoa, your arm has been shot," Officer Cutler said.

"Yeah, we are being hunted by two crazy people right now," Corey said.

"I'll call the paramedics for that arm in just a sec," Officer Cutler said. Then, to the rest of us, "Does anyone know the names of these people?"

"Dr. Truex and Bruce," I said. "There's also a guy named Enzo, but he's still in the place we escaped from."

"What place?" he asked.

"The place with the White Room," Milly said.

Officer Cutler took his glasses off and placed them in his shirt pocket. He produced a pen and pad for writing notes. "Walk with me back to my cruiser. It's not too far from here."

We followed Officer Cutler and told him about almost everything that took place in the White Room. The sage-green room where they housed us. All the odd jobs they made me do. By the time we reached his cruiser, he knew the salient parts of the story.

Beyond his cruiser, perhaps fifty or sixty yards, was the hard road. It appeared that he had driven through a narrow opening in the woods and parked his car in a small area that wasn't as cluttered with trees as the rest of the woods.

Officer Cutler pointed ahead at the narrow opening by the road. "I run radar out here all the time. That's one of my go-to spots. It's a good thing I had my window down. That's how I heard you yelling out there. People have been looking for you guys for some time now."

"Really? Like search teams?" I asked.

"Yeah, but we had an extremely difficult time finding any leads. Now, let me call the paramedics for this boy's arm." Officer Cutler pulled a cell phone out of his pocket and looked back at us. "This will be quicker than calling it in over the radio."

Corey, Zane, and I turned around to keep an eye out for Bruce and Dr. Truex. We began to talk about how we had escaped from that facility out in the middle of the woods, how we overcame the odds and didn't die in the White Room like so many had before us. We were happy to be alive but sad for all of those who were not as fortunate.

"How's your arm, Core?" I asked.

"Feels like it's on fire," he said. "I'm getting tired, too. Just drained from all that running, I guess."

"I hope those paramedics get here soon," Zane said. "You're starting to get kind of pale, Corey."

"I'll be fine, guys."

"Tell me if you start to feel worse, okay," I said.

He nodded. Then we heard Milly say something from behind us. She was still looking at Officer Cutler, who had just ended his phone call. "Jonah," she whispered in a trembling voice.

"What's wrong, Milly?"

When she turned to face me, her eyes were large, dilated, and full of terror. She struggled to say these next words. They came out shaky and barely audible, but I heard them. "He's one of them."

Chapter 24

By the look of her, I could tell she had read Officer Cutler's mind. And thank God she had.

Right then, I began thinking of ways to get us away from this man. Only problem was that this guy had a gun, taser, and years of training. But if we could play it cool and not let him know that we were privy to his plan, we'd be able to catch him off guard.

I hugged Milly and whispered in her ear, "I have a plan. Just be casual."

"She okay?" Officer Cutler asked while walking back toward us.

"Yeah, she's fine," I said. "She just really wants to see her parents again."

Officer Cutler bent down to be at eye level with Milly, then said, "Don't worry, kiddo. You'll see your parents in no time."

I saw him wink at her, and it sickened me. After watching his little act, it was clear to me what his true intentions were. Milly was right about him. He was one of *them* and was probably getting a percentage of the money earned from every organ sold.

I didn't wait another second to execute my plan. I twisted around, looking in the woods. "Did you guys hear that?"

"Hear what?" Corey and Zane asked. It was good that they didn't know what Milly and I knew about Officer Cutler. It made deceiving him that much easier.

Officer Cutler's face twisted into a frown. "What'd you hear?"

"I think it might be the crazy people who chased us out here. The ones who locked us in cells," I said, trying to sound frightened.

"Wait here," Officer Cutler said, creeping past us to investigate.

As soon as he went past me, I bent down to retrieve one of the syringes full of Midazolam. Corey and Zane watched me lift the syringe out of my sock, confused and scared. I put my finger to my lips to indicate that I needed them to be quiet. Then I whispered, "Milly said he's one of them. After I inject him with this, we have to hold him down until the drug has time to work."

Corey shook his head, unafraid and ready to fight.

Zane was dismayed by what I had said but also knew what he had to do.

Then to Milly, I whispered, "If this goes bad, run."

I sidled up behind Officer Cutler with Zane and Corey in my wake. I was careful not to step on any leaves or sticks that might ruin our plan, but Zane wasn't. I was only five feet from Cutler when Zane stepped on a stick, cracking and breaking it. The cop spun around and found me charging him with a syringe. One of his hands caught my wrist. The other caught me by the throat. He headbutted me hard enough to make me almost lose consciousness. My vision became blurry for a short time, but I saw Zane and Corey rush Officer Cutler while I was trying to regain my vision and balance. Then I realized I had dropped the syringe. I sat there watching nebulous versions of Zane and Corey fight with Officer Cutler. Slowly, my vision was coming back.

As Cutler was throwing Zane aside, Corey tackled him to the ground. Zane rushed back over and grabbed one of his arms while Corey tried to hold the other. They were calling for me to help, but I was still disoriented from receiving the blow to my head. A few seconds later, as I sat there, unable to stand up without falling back over, Milly came running up to me. She lifted my pant leg, grabbed the syringe out of my sock, and, while the cop was concerned with Zane and Corey, jabbed the needle into his neck and injected him with the knockout drug. In mere seconds, Officer Cutler lost consciousness.

"Holy crap, Milly. Way to go," Corey said, fist-bumping her with his good arm.

"I'm just glad you didn't listen to Jonah and stuck around," Zane said.

Milly looked up at them and smiled. "I couldn't leave you guys. Not after everything we've been through. I feel safer with all of you." Then she turned to me. "Come on. Let's go help Jonah. He's unable to stand right now. That headbutt really did a number on him."

She wasn't exaggerating, either. (I still have the scar just above my eyebrow to prove it.)

Once my vision came back completely, I noticed something I hadn't before. I felt something running down my face. I touched it with the tips of my fingers and found that I was bleeding. It trickled down from the cut Officer Cutler'd made by striking me with his forehead.

"Damn, are you okay?" Corey asked me.

"I'll be fine. You're the one with the gunshot wound," I said. "Quick, one of you grab his phone and call nine-one-one. Have them trace us by his car or something."

"I'm on it," Zane said, rushing over to the cop. First, he took Cutler's Glock from him and handed it to me. "Here, Jonah. You've shot a gun before, haven't you?"

"I have," I said. "I begged my dad to take me to the shooting range after I turned eighteen."

Then Zane dug around in Cutler's pockets and held up the cop's cell phone. He dialed 911 and looked at us while he waited for someone to answer. Zane's eyes lit up when he heard the voice on the other end of the line. We listened as he went on to tell them our location, what had happened to us, and that they could pinpoint us by using either Cutler's cell phone or his police car. The lady on the phone wanted him to stay on the line. She had more questions. But Zane hung up. He took a deep breath and looked at me. "How was that?"

"Good enough for government work, I suppose," I said. "They should be able to find us now. We just have to—"

"Don't move. Any of you."

I knew that voice, and it made my stomach churn.

"Thought you could run away, didn't you, string bean?" Bruce asked while pointing his gun at us. "Yep. You all thought you could run away."

"You are all in very big trouble! When we get you back to the lab, every single one of you will experience the most painful surgery of your lives. I guarantee it!" Dr. Truex yelled, pointing at us as if we were the bad guys. "All we were trying to do is help you little cretins. I was trying to come up with a cure. I'll still do that, but now it's going to hurt. Every little thing I do to you will hurt. And if anyone tries to run away, I've instructed Bruce to shoot that person. We aren't playing games anymore. You disobey, you die. Have I made myself clear?"

I was so focused on hiding my gun and listening to Dr. Truex that I didn't notice that Corey had left us. I was clueless about when he left, where he went to, and how he did it so quietly. I wanted to look around for him, but I couldn't with Bruce and Dr. Truex closing in on us. I had the gun, but Bruce had his trained on me, Milly, and Zane. Knowing that I wouldn't be able to draw quick enough, I waited to be captured. I was all out of plans.

As they got closer to us, Dr. Truex said, "Bruce, wait." She looked to the left and right of where we were standing. "Where's the other one?"

"The other what?"

"The boy. Where's the other—"

Above their heads was a myriad of tree branches covered with leaves. Corey was hiding in there, his body almost completely concealed by foliage. My brother jumped on top of Bruce and knocked him to the ground. His gun fell out of his hand and near Dr. Truex's feet. She snatched it up and aimed it at Corey before I could bring my pistol up from where I had been hiding it.

She fired twice.

Chapter 25

Two flashes appeared from the gun's barrel. The sound it made when it discharged was deafening to the point that I could only hear a strange whining noise ringing in my head. Bruce was starting to get up from the ground, and Corey lay there holding his neck.

I felt my eyes beginning to water. Before I knew it, and before Dr. Truex could turn around to shoot the rest of us, my gun was aimed at her. I held it tight in both hands and, as blood from the gash continued to trickle down my face, squeezed the trigger repeatedly. More deafening gunshots rang in my head as I saw little red holes appear on Dr. Truex's mid-section. I had hit my target, and she hit the ground.

I began to cry. Not because I had shot and killed an evil person, but because Corey had risked his life for us and was on the ground, clutching his neck where he had been shot. I knew I was losing my brother as the seconds passed.

Through my tears, I saw Bruce glance several times between me and Dr. Truex. He put his hands up, breathing heavily, a look of disbelief across his face. It was strange seeing him look at me that way, and I wanted to shoot him. I was sure he could tell that I did. I aimed the Glock at him and put pressure on the trigger.

"Jonah, wait," Milly said.

"Why should I? They killed Corey!"

"They tried to, Jonah, but they didn't," she said.

I glanced down and saw Corey still moving. He was trying to get up. "Zane, check on Corey. Bruce, if you move a muscle, you're dead."

Bruce stood completely still, his hands in the air. "Easy, string bean. Just put the gun down. No one else has to die."

"If you call me string bean again, I'll shoot you in the leg," I said. "Maybe both of them."

He must have realized just how serious I was, because that was the last time he ever addressed me by that stupid nickname.

I kept the gun on Bruce while Zane helped Corey sit up. The first bullet had grazed Corey's neck. He was bleeding a little, but he was okay. The handgun's recoil had made Dr. Truex miss him entirely on the second shot. It was lodged in the dirt twelve inches from his head.

"Am I okay, Zane? It burns," Corey said.

"I think so, man. It just grazed you from what I can tell."

Corey grinned a little, then met my eyes, and the grin disappeared. It must have been the tears he saw still resting on my cheeks or the blood running down my face. Either way, I thought that I had lost my little brother. I thought my world had been changed forever. I'd thought about what my dad would think if he knew Corey had died because he came looking for me. A lot of things had crossed my mind just then.

Around the time Corey sat up and saw me holding the gun I had pointed at Bruce, I heard sirens in the distance. They had tracked us from the 911 call we'd made and were coming toward us fast. Soon, the sirens got louder and louder.

"Jonah, he's thinking about running," Milly said.

Bruce looked at Milly, his face twisted in rage. "She's lying. She's a damn liar."

I smiled at him. "Bruce, she's a big part of why I'm here holding this gun and you're there waiting to go to prison. She's not lying. She can hear what you're thinking."

"That's impossible, string—Jonah. You expect me to believe that garbage?"

"I don't care if you do or— Stop!"

Bruce lunged to his left and dove for Corey. I fired three times, missing twice but hitting his upper right thigh with one round. Despite the gunshot wound, he grabbed Corey and Zane around their necks, squeezing tight while screaming like a mad man. I ran over to shoot him, but he had placed Corey and Zane on top of him. They were squirming, and I couldn't get a clear shot. Now Bruce was smiling at me. The police were close, but I didn't think they'd find us in time.

"You either let me go or I kill them. What's it going to be, kid?"

Their faces were past red and beginning to turn purple.

"Fine!" I said. "Just let them go!"

"Oh no," Bruce said. "You back up, drop the gun, and I'll keep these two as cover. Don't worry. I'll drop them as soon as I get to the edge of the woods."

"Okay, then go!"

From behind me, Milly said, "He's lying. He plans to kill them, Jonah."

She said it so softly that Bruce didn't hear her. And now that I was privy to Bruce's true intentions, I had to chance shooting him and accidentally hitting my best friend or my brother. Once again, I had no choice. They'd die if I didn't try.

I dropped the gun a few feet in front of me. As soon as it hit the dirt, Bruce sprung to his feet, one arm still wrapped tightly around Corey, the other wrapped just as tightly around Zane. He ran, hardly limping at all, even with the bullet lodged deep into the muscle of his thigh. I reached down for the gun as he ran toward the woods, but when I looked up to fire the Glock, I saw that Bruce had stopped running.

In front of Bruce were seven police officers. Two had their firearms trained at his head while the other five charged him. Bruce released Corey and Zane, and then he attempted to take on the five officers. He threw the first one to the side. The second knocked him over, and the other three pinned him to the ground.

On the road in front of us, more cops were running into the woods. I dropped the Glock and ran over to check on Corey and Zane. They were unconscious.

I yelled, "We need paramedics!"

One of the police officers used his walkie to bring the medics in. I watched them run from the road as fast as they could. There were three of them, and the two who reached us first began mouth-to-mouth resuscitation immediately. I watched helplessly as they worked on Corey and Zane until a few police officers took Milly and me off to the side.

"Come on. You two don't need to see this," one of them told us.

I let them drag us away, mostly because I felt weak and defeated even though I had made it out of those woods alive. I couldn't stop crying.

Milly and I were sitting in the back of an ambulance. They were asking us questions as they cleaned the blood off my face and examined the gash above my eye. I wasn't paying any attention to their questions, though. All I could think about were my brother and Zane.

The paramedic realized I wasn't listening or answering any of the questions. She retrieved some disinfectant and a butterfly bandage from her bag, then said, "I'm just going to clean up the gash and put this bandage on for now. When we get you to the hospital, they'll stitch it up." Then she shifted her gaze to Milly. "I'm sorry about all of the questions, but I have to ask them. I can't imagine what you've all been through." She met my eyes again. "I'll save the questions for later, okay?"

From behind her, a police officer called her over, and she left us.

Milly grabbed my hand. She knew what I was thinking. She knew I was blaming myself for not being able to save Corey and Zane from Bruce. She knew it all. And then she gave me a hug and said, "You can't blame yourself. You did your best, Jonah." Then she let go of me, and her expression changed. She appeared to be happy, even as tears ran down her face.

"Milly, are you okay?" I asked.

She was staring at the ambulance's window next to me as if she were hypnotized. Then she turned around to look at the police officers and paramedics coming out of the woods where they had tackled Bruce.

"Milly, what's going on?"

After a hesitation, she glanced back at me as the wind blew her disheveled hair from her face. She said, "They're alive."

I tried to keep my voice under control, but it cracked when I said, "Are you...sure?"

She reached for my hand, and I gave it to her. "Come on. They're wondering where you are."

We walked quickly down the little path into the woods, where Corey and Zane were still on the ground, surrounded by paramedics and police officers. To my right, I saw four police officers escorting Bruce out of the woods and to the back of one of the police cars. He was no longer trying to fight them. He had given up. I thought about how funny it was seeing him in handcuffs when he was so fond of slapping cuffs on all of our wrists.

I jogged over to the group of first responders and saw my brother and best friend lying on the ground still. And just as Milly had said, they were alive. I used my shirt to wipe the tears from my face and kneeled next to Corey, Zane, and the paramedics while Milly stood behind me, the palm of her hand resting on my shoulder. Before I could say anything, one of the paramedics asked me whose idea it was to put the tourniquet on Corey's arm.

"It was my idea," I said, worried I had done something terribly wrong by doing so.

"Well," the paramedic said, "it could have been pretty bad if you hadn't suggested to put a tourniquet on his arm. Even though the bullet wound isn't bleeding at an alarming rate, he could have eventually still bled out without the proper medical attention. You pretty much saved his life, kid."

The paramedic smiled at me and glanced over at Corey and Zane. "I'll be right back with some stretchers. You guys sit tight and don't try to move, okay?"

They both gave the paramedic a thumbs up, then shifted their eyes over toward me when the first responder went to get the stretchers.

"Hey, big bro, we were wondering where you went," Corey said.

"Yeah, man, they wouldn't tell us if you were okay or not at first," Zane said.

Hearing their voices at that moment made me happier than I thought I had ever been before in my life. It didn't seem real that the four of us had made it out of that place alive, especially considering so many others had not. I did what felt right in that moment: I bent down and wrapped my arms around each of them until the paramedics came back.

Chapter 26

As Corey and Zane were being loaded into ambulances, something came stumbling into my mind like a drunk leaving the bar at last call. I had been so distraught and worried about Corey and Zane that I had completely forgotten about Officer Cutler and Enzo. Without delay, I found the closet cop I could find and told him the story and where they were. Soon after, I watched as three police officers carried Officer Cutler's limp body past us. I imagined his face when he woke up to a detective questioning him about his involvement with Dr. Truex. If only I could be a fly on that wall.

Shortly after that, Milly and I rode in the back of a police car to the hospital that Corey and Zane were being transported to. When we arrived, I was taken to a room to have the gash above my eye stitched up, and Milly was taken into a separate room for an exam. She didn't want to be split up at first—and I knew why—but I assured her that everything would be fine.

After they took care of the gash above my eye and asked me three dozen questions, I told them I wanted to see my brother and Zane. I was led to a room that wasn't too far from the one they had stitched me up in. Milly was already in there, sitting down in a chair. She smiled when she saw me and said, "Guys, Jonah's here."

There were two beds, and Corey and Zane occupied them. It was apparent that Corey had been given some kind of pain killer, because his eyes were half-lidded and he was breathing slowly.

Zane saw me looking at my brother. He said, "Hey, dude, they gave Corey something for pain. They're doing surgery on him soon, I guess. They said the bullet is still in his arm."

"Yeah, he seems a bit out of it," I said, then glanced up at Zane. "What about you? You okay?"

"I'm just glad to be out of that place and in a real hospital. I still can't believe we made it out of there."

"Jonah?" Corey said. He was lying down with his head turned toward me.

"Yeah, Core, it's me."

"Who's that behind you?"

I turned around slowly and found my dad looking at me from the door's threshold. There were tears in his eyes and a few running down his cheeks. I said, "Don't worry. Corey's okay, Dad."

He walked up and threw his arms around me. I didn't remember ever embracing like that with my old man before. Even when Mom had died, he had never held me so tight. "I've been a mess not knowing if you boys were alive or dead. I thought I lost you. I thought I lost you both," he said.

"We're okay, Dad," Corey said from his bed. "Just a couple scratches."

"Milly," a nurse said from the hall.

"Yes," Milly replied.

"I have some people here who would like to see—"

She knew who was out there. Her ability told her before the nurse could. Milly jumped up before the nurse could finish talking and ran into the arms of her mother and father. I watched as they held their daughter, crying, so happy to not have lost her forever. At some point, Milly glanced back at me, smiling from ear to ear. I smiled back and thought, *Take care, Milly.*

You, too, she mouthed back, then walked down the hall holding her parents' hands. About a minute later, I saw a man on crutches enter the room. His left leg was wrapped up to his upper thigh in some sort of cast. I blinked a few times and was looking at who I thought was a dead man.

"Mr. Bosworth," he said. "I heard you were here. I'm glad to see you're still on this side of the dirt."

"I could say the same to you, Officer Welkins. How—"

"How am I still alive? Well, when those guys hit me with their car, I went flying into the woods, or so I'm told. The impact not only broke my leg, but it also knocked me unconscious and broke a few ribs. I remember talking to you, and that's it. Everything went black until they found me. Here's the thing. I don't even remember why I pulled you over in the first place."

"He was driving me home because I was too drunk to drive. He was saving my ass," Corey said from behind me.

I smiled at my brother and looked back at Officer Welkins. "I just didn't want Corey to make a mistake that could cost him his future. Better me than him."

A grin appeared on Officer Welkins's chiseled face. "You know, kid, that's commendable. But what's really commendable is what I was told about how you helped get those kids out of that horrible place and bring down those terrible people. I can't begin to tell you how impressed I am. Anyway, I came here to tell you not to worry about those charges. You've been through a lot, as have I. My advice to you, Mr. Bosworth, is to recover from this, just as I am going to recover from what has happened to me. You understand?"

I did. He meant that I shouldn't dwell on all the bad things that had happened to me in that place. I understood...but I would never forget. I'd never forget Ronnie or the boy he told me about, nor would it slip my mind how we were treated. Some of us were beaten, and all of us were waiting for our death sentences. I'd never forget a lot of things. But most of all, beyond anything, I would never forget the feeling I got every time I entered the White Room. The feeling of not knowing if I'd make it back out alive.

Epilogue

Even four years later, it's still hard to believe. I learned that being captured, beaten, and nearly killed by psychopaths does change a person. Who would have guessed, right?

I no longer ride a motorcycle. The urge just isn't there. I feel like every person has a limited supply of luck, and I used most of mine up escaping that place with only a few bruises and a gash above my eye. The scar is still prominent above my eyebrow. I see it every time I look in the mirror.

I went to only one court hearing. It was nice to see Bruce, Enzo, and the recently terminated Officer Cutler in orange jumpsuits. At one point during the hearing, they all scowled at us, and I don't know about the others, but it made my stomach churn. But when the hearing was over, that feeling in my gut was gone. In its place was relief, because the judge had given the three of them life in prison.

I never went back to work for Larry Ashmore, but I did thank him for what he had taught me. Knowing how to fix certain things had kept me alive and helped me get out of a situation I had thought was impossible to get out of. Milly was a big part of it, of course, as were Corey and Zane. Without Milly's ability, I wouldn't be here. None of us would.

I wanted to learn more about fixing things, primarily electrical issues. After working as an apprentice and getting my license, I became an electrician. The pay is good, the work is steady, and most days I even enjoy doing the work.

I have a wife now, a baby on the way, and my own house a couple miles from my dad's. I wanted to stay close to him because he's getting older and lives alone. Dad is doing okay, though. He enjoys when we invite him over for dinner once a week. When he comes over, we talk about Corey, of course. He is always worrying about him up in Tennessee.

Corey got a full-ride scholarship to play baseball for the Tennessee Volunteers. It took a full year for his left arm to heal from being shot. He says it's a lot better, but not exactly what it used to be. Luckily for him, he's a righty and not a lefty. The injury never impeded his ability to swing the hell out of a bat. The kid has hit three homeruns this year already—the most on his team.

Zane just got hired on with the local fire department a few months ago and tells me he is loving it. After he started the academy all those months ago, I haven't seen him a whole lot, but we make a point to go to the skatepark a few times a year just to roll around like we used to. And even though we don't see each other as much, he's still my best friend.

I haven't seen Milly since that last court hearing. She and her parents moved up to Tallahassee a few months after the hearing was finished. They just never felt safe in this area after what happened. We still talk on the phone now and then. She is in her freshman year of high school and doing well. She still has her ability to read people's minds. I asked her if she had put any thought into what she wants to do after high school. She told me she was thinking about studying law enforcement and specializing in police interrogation.

After we all left the hospital four years ago, we were given a phone number for a psychologist with the name Bill Streetman. I know Milly, Corey, and Zane no longer talk to him. They've moved on and left most of it behind them, which is good. I've left a lot of it behind, as well, but some of it still haunts me when I go to rest my head at night. Sometimes I dream of Ronnie playing with his cards in the corner of my bedroom, coughing up blood. Even the unbidden image of bullet holes in Dr. Truex's mid-section gets stuck in my mind every so often.

And if I catch a whiff of anything resembling the scent of coconuts, the urge to run to my car and leave where I am becomes almost insurmountable. For those reasons, I continue to talk with Bill and have lunch with him from time to time. I stay focused on the positive things in my life, as he urges me to do. I've learned to live with it, as many others have had to do with tragedies they've endured. I've never been back to that long stretch of two-lane blacktop, not since that ride in the back of a police car with Milly.

Tomorrow, my wife and I will pick my father up from his house. We will drive to the airport and fly to Tennessee to visit Corey. To get there, we have to take that long stretch of two-lane blacktop where I was tricked, drugged, and taken. It's that or take an alternate route that will take considerably longer, which I have done time and time again. I've avoided that road for years now, but this morning my mom's words filled my mind, and I knew it was time to face it. Her words were kind, but this time what she said was a little different than normal.

You can do this, Jonah. Live your life, honey. It's just a road, after all.

Acknowledgments

I would like to thank my friend, Sue Harmon, for answering my many questions, encouraging me, and helping me become a better writer. Also, I would like to thank my friends and family that have supported me along the way.